Durable

Book I

By Saugia N. Smiley

[signature]

To the awesome flight attendant that made a long flight Awesome

Edited by
C.S. Smiley, YPRS INC!

Cover Photo & Design
Laeeq Hussain Arif

Published by Saugia N. Smiley
An imprint of Saugia N. Smiley
411 Highland Cross Drive, Houston, TX 77073

Request use of material from this book
by email: smilesdarkskin@gmail.com
by mail: YPR INC! c/o C.S. Smiley
PO Box 692770, Quincy, MA 02269

ISBN 978-1-7339058-0-0

Contents

Acknowledgments

To my mother, you have always encouraged me to follow my dreams and to be the best version of myself. Your unwavering support was evident as you read and even re-read chapter after chapter of this book. Thank you!

I would also like to thank YPRS, INC! my editing firm and specifically my dedicated editor for not quitting on me when I went into hyper writing mode and made significant changes close to the publication deadline.

Finally, I would like to thank you, Manual Goody, for being the push I needed to finally publish my books.

Prologue

And So It Begins…
The Kingdom of Corentha, 2000 years ago

The subtle fragrance of orchids wafted through the hall growing stronger as I drew closer to my destination. Apprehension clung to me, a dragging weight on my every step.

A storm brewed behind my moss-colored eyes as I recalled how elated the maid in the courtyard had been as she informed us that she had decorated the throne room for Princess Iris' wedding that morning. For a second, I stood there frozen in shock as I digested what I had heard, thinking *"that's not possible."* Without a second thought, I took off in the direction of the throne room barely registering all the calls for me to come back.

I would pay dearly for leaving my post, but if Iris, my Iris, was getting married I needed to see for myself. I was her mate!

Only a few hours ago she had laid in my arms and told me that she was pregnant with my baby. Now she was to be married?! I couldn't believe it, wouldn't believe it. She would never betray me this way. My eyes turned to slits at the distant sound of trumpets behind the large solid silver and red doors ahead.

I was steps away from the doors when they flung open with a flourish, and a scarlet floor length tulle ball gown swept over the entrance. Caught off guard, I followed my warrior's instincts, immediately backed away and melted into the shadows of the hallway. As I stood watching, over the threshold stepped a head of auburn hair in an intricate up-do with a few loose strands of hair framing a heart-shaped face with twinkling blue eyes and a smattering of freckles across a small button nose.

Blood red rubies dripped from her ears and neck portraying an elegance only attributable to royalty. It took a moment to realize that the woman standing before me, arms linked with Gitto Bernadotte, was my mate. Gitto was decked out in the kingdom's traditional wedding wear. I had never seen it before, there hadn't been a new king in about five centuries, but my mother had described it to me. Between the white lapels and the red decorative flowers flowing from the shoulders to the waist, I knew precisely what it was. As if I needed any more confirmation, they were wearing matching crowns signifying marriage and a coronation.

The blood from my recent feed rushed up the full length of my body sending my slow beating heart into a gallop. Icy winds of delirious anger, insanity, and torment swept over me as I watched them smile and bow completing the last rite of passage that would lead them to the throne. The ache in my heart intensified as they turned as one and walked back towards the throne room to take their place as the new King and Queen of the vampire race.

I opened my mouth to scream in defiance, but a crippling pain surged over me forcing me out of the shadows making me visible to nearby bystanders. A sharp gasp sounded a few feet ahead of me and I knew without looking that Iris was experiencing the same feeling.

Paralysis and confusion flittered in my mind until I realized that it was the breaking of our mate-bond. In marrying Gitto, Iris had ripped apart the bond meant to keep us together.

Drawing a deep breath, I climbed to my feet just as her husband helped her up and our eyes met and locked. In hers, there was a flash of happiness, agony, bewilderment, and then, finally, disgust.

The latter blew me away. Up until that moment, I had hoped that this was just a prank or, if it was real, she was under duress but that look, that look cemented everything for me. An uncontrollable strangled groan bubbled pass my lips as another spasm of pain rose and spread through me while the last remnants of our bond dissolved.

A smile of contempt on her face, Iris gestured to the man by her side that she was okay and they should proceed. With purpose-filled steps and a sick look of glee in her eyes, Queen Iris maintained eye contact with me as she and her King stepped into the throne room and the door slammed shut.

Fury erupted, gushing like a geyser that had been blocked for far too long. A sickening smile of my own glided unto my face and I bowed in mockery of their rites and turned away from everything that was the vampire kingdom of Corentha.

With a dark chuckle born of hate, despair, and ridicule I melted back into the shadows. A plan to bring everything in this kingdom to its knees already brewing in my mind.

1992

"One. Two. Three. Push!!" Searing pain tore through her body as the experiment inside of her struggled to make its way into the world. It felt like someone had set her insides on fire. She struggled to breathe amidst the anguish while hate permeated her mind and her soul. The husband that she used to hold so dear had volunteered her body for this; now instead of standing by her side, he stood alongside the other scientists staring down at her from the observation deck.

To make matters worse, the doctors and nurses surrounding her appeared more concerned about the experiment's health than hers. "One more time" they chanted. "One. Two. Three. Now push!!!" Summoning all the hatred and disdain that had built up over the past five months, Sue-Ann bore down and pushed with all her might. There was a sucking noise, and relief flooded her body at the sound of a baby's wail ringing through the dastardly room. In her moment of relief, she had focused her energy on catching her breath and almost missed the muted gasps of surprise.

She was on the verge of panic but felt reassured seconds later as her snake of a husband came bursting into the room; a look of awe on his face. The look of wonder quickly gave way to one of sly triumph as he took the child from one of the nurses. Sue-Ann couldn't help but glare at the happy glint in her husband's eyes.

Her resentment threatened to take over and she had an urge to beat him into the floor. "This is unexpected, but promising!" Laughing maniacally, Peter walked over to his wife and lowered the tightly bundled baby so that she could see her for the first time.

She gasped just like the doctors and nurses had only seconds ago. She glanced up at her husband and in a voice saturated with fear stuttered, "th-th-this shouldn't be possible!" Looking up at her, with eyes only a few shades darker than her own, was a face nearly identical to hers.

*****

As he used the security camera to zoom in on the face of the wailing baby, moss-colored eyes flashed with triumphant madness. His dream was finally a reality! His greatest creation was here and with her birth his revenge was nigh.

Chapter 1

A Devastating Blow

Graduation was a week away, and all her classes were finished but they had given her the option to come in, and she had taken it. Unfortunately, there were no sports scheduled after the last bell, so she had to go home.

Humming to herself, seventeen year old Nicolette Winspere, known to her friends as Nikki, skipped through the front door of the two-family house she had called home for as long as she could remember. As she stepped through the door, Tito from the first floor began to bark, an invitation that typically drew her in, but today her stomach drove her up the stairs to her door.

Pale green walls and a wave of sadness greeted her as she stepped into the kitchen. There was no comfort in being home and not for the first time this week she wished there was an after-school activity so she could stay away a little longer.

Another growl from her tummy reminded her why she was in the kitchen. With a sigh, she did the robotic task of making herself a sandwich while her mind wandered.

College was right around the corner, and she was ecstatic. She just wished her family would share her happiness. Instead, she felt as though their hatred for her had intensified. For as long as she could remember she had felt alone. The older she got, the more her mother seemed to despise her and lately her father had been giving her that same look of permanent disdain.

When she was younger, she had been so distraught over being rejected that she had researched it for hours but could never actually find any explanation for her mother's behavior. Sighing again, this time in exasperation, she shook her head getting rid of her miserable thoughts; after all, it was too late now; she was getting ready to leave this house forever. Just as she was biting into her sandwich, she glimpsed the time on the digital clock over the fridge and realized that her mother was due home any minute.

As if on cue, the stairs began to creak from both downstairs and upstairs and her siblings came rushing by her. Nikki backed up quickly to avoid getting run over.

Sucking in a deep breath, Nikki tried to minimize her presence but at 5'5", with dark skin, smoldering mud oak eyes, long, lean legs accentuated by years of playing tennis, and an eye-catching smile, it was almost impossible. Although, over the years she had mastered the art of making herself invisible.

The front door swung open with a loud "pop," and an ominous shiver ran down Nikki's spine as her mother stepped into the room. Shouts of "Mommy!" and "Hi, Mother" filled the kitchen as the kids waited a beat to gauge their mother's response before throwing themselves at her. Two of the four attacked her with hugs and kisses while the older two stood back and greeted her from afar.

Nicolette stared at the older version of herself, who was identical in every way and swallowed hard. It always unnerved her when her own face looked back at her with so much animosity. Over time she had learned to avoid making eye contact with her mother as well as looking in mirrors.

Sue-Ann Winspere, known to her friends as Suzy, was beautiful, and she knew it.

Confidence and sex appeal oozed from her like a fragrance masking the burning aversion she harbored for her eldest daughter.

Looking around, she surveyed her "eggs," as she liked to call them, before mumbling a brief greeting and heading upstairs to her room.

A sigh from all four children was the only indication that they had been nervous but, she was happy so they were okay.

Turning back to her sandwich, Nikki ignored her siblings and they, in turn, ignored her. They had been taught at a young age to give her a wide berth.

Though they might have feared their mother, they would never speak to her about it or include her in any plans of dissent. In fact, they made sure that she was blamed for everything, whether it was her fault or theirs. She wasn't stupid, and she was sure her parents weren't either, but they preferred to punish her regardless of who was at fault.

That thought in mind, she followed behind her mother up the old, creaking, stairs and entered her room. She still had a few last-minute college applications to fill out.

*****

"Nicolette!!" The hollering of her name seemed to echo and bounce around in her head, waking her from a deep sleep. She knew what was coming, but she still hurled herself out of bed and down the stairs. When she reached the bottom of the staircase, she could feel herself becoming angry. Seeds of fear began to bloom, as well. Fear turned to terror however, when she saw her mother's face twisted with rage and hate.

In a flash, Nicolette was yanked by the arm and just as swiftly her face was shoved into the kitchen counter. Above her, she could hear her mother's strangled voice as she growled her frustrations.

"What is this?! How many times must I tell you to clean up after yourself?! You are practically eighteen and leaving a mess wherever you go. So damned disgusting! I can't wait until next week when you aren't my problem anymore. No longer will you be a blight on this family. I will finally be rid of you for good!"

Rage pumped through her veins and a perverse sense of victory bloomed in her heart as Sue-Ann grabbed Nicolette and threw her to the ground. "You have been nothing but a disappointing cancer to this family. You are unworthy of existing and today I will make you feel all the pain you have caused me over the years." Pulling back her leg, she rained down kicks of fury on her first born child. She did not attempt to soften the blows nor cared where they landed.

Typically, she aimed low, where the bruises would be hidden. However, now that school was out she had no reason to show restraint. Two, three, then four minutes passed and still the kicks continued in near silence except for a few grunts from Sue-Ann. Nikki was used to this having been through beatings, in the past, so brutal that she had been forced to stay home. She didn't remember when it had started, but it happened often enough that by the time she was thirteen years old she had learned the unwritten rules of these encounters with her mother.

The louder she was, the longer it went on; the quieter she was, the stronger the blows. To protect herself, she had learned to create a place in her head where she heard and saw everything but felt nothing. She would hiss in pain at the appropriate times and cried at others solely for her mother's benefit.

It seemed endless but after almost 10 minutes Sue-Ann grew tired, and with one final kick she hauled Nicolette up and shoved her to the sink. "Clean this shit up and quickly!" Stomping to the fridge, Sue-Ann spun and surveyed her handy work. She could see the bruises already setting in, and it pleased her immensely. A cruel grin graced her beautiful face as she turned and walked away. It wouldn't be long before the experiment would be leaving, permanently.

Years of conditioning had taught Nicolette not to protest or even to bother trying to explain herself in these situations. Instead, she moved as quickly as her body allowed and washed the dishes before putting them away neatly. Tears fell from her eyes as she registered the pain her body radiated. Her stomach felt as though it had been turned inside out but she never made a sound. Easing her way up the stairs as quietly as she could, she said a silent prayer, hoping that she would make it to her room without running into her mother again.

By some miracle she made it to the top of the stairs without a problem and was almost to her room when the unexpected happened: she heard her father's voice. She had always been a daddy's girl, at least up until two years ago. It was right after another test in the lab of hell, that the look in his eyes had started to change. Now he looked at her as though she were nothing more than an annoyance. It hadn't bothered her too much at first because she was sure that whatever she had done to upset him she could make it better.

She expected a lot of things from her mother. In fact, nothing she did surprised Nicolette anymore. Her father, however, he was her strength. He was the one person she used to keep herself grounded when her mother's wrath was too much to bear. She was sure of him, so she never bothered to build any defenses against him, but his next words made her wish she had. "I wish we could have gotten rid of her sooner but..."

Anything else he said was drowned out by the thumping of her heart as it tried to beat out her chest. Stumbling through her bedroom door, she barely took two steps in before crumpling to the floor. A burning tingle spread from her arm up to her heart activating a flow of twin rivers from her eyes to her cheeks. Her mind rejected it, but her heart felt and recognized it forcing her mind to come to the conclusion that her father, the man she adored, couldn't wait to be rid of her. Hope slipped from her grasp and in its place an emptiness arose.

There was a pop in her ears as though she were on a plane that had just landed. Something within her awakened and the most peculiar sensation of pins and needles ran through her as everything became clear. She could see and understand everything, and it was painfully obvious that her time in this place was finished.

With a speed she didn't know she possessed, Nicolette stood up and dove into the back of her closet for her knapsack that contained money, snacks, and clothes. She had been preparing for this moment ever since the night that woman had locked her out the house in nothing but her nightgown.

From then on, she worked small odd jobs around the neighborhood and saved every penny. Whirling towards the door, Nicolette snagged her sneakers, yanked the door open, and seemed to flash down the stairs. She was almost out the door when someone bellowed her name, but she didn't pause, didn't look back, just pumped her legs faster needing to lose herself in another type of pain.

Chapter 2

Where to Hide?

The harsh slapping of her feet echoed against the cold pavement in the quiet of the night. The sound was muted to her ears by her painful gasps for air as she pumped her legs faster. She relished the pain that shot up her legs and into her body as it drowned out the ache in her heart. She had tried so hard to be a good daughter, but she couldn't; not anymore.

Her soul was dying! Another day, no another minute, in that house and she would lose the will to live. For years she had struggled to maintain her spirits using any and everything at her disposal. A smile from her teacher, a hug from her friends, a pat on the back from her father, even a laugh with that woman but it hadn't been enough and tonight, tonight, had been her breaking point. Two weeks to her eighteenth birthday, only a week before graduation, and she had lost the war.

Her legs ate up the ground in front of her until they burned unbearably, and she almost stumbled to the ground. Eyes roving, Nicolette searched for a place to sit, desperate to rest her burning limbs. She noticed a bench a few meters ahead and with trembling legs she collapsed gracelessly onto her back.

Her ragged breathing seemed to fill the empty night as she waited for her heart to slow down and her mind to start working again.

As she laid there gazing up a bout of despair washed over her, and she wondered if her life was destined to be as dark and empty as the night sky. Afraid of her thoughts, Nicolette shook her head and focused on her surroundings. To her right, she was surprised to find that she recognized the row of old Victorian-era houses. There was only one place she knew that had those houses across from them and it was the train station.

With a start she sat up, eyes filled with amazement, as she spotted the familiar tattered sign with the T symbol on it. Somehow, she had managed to run a standard thirty-minute car ride from her home to the train station.

For a moment panic surged as the gravity of what she had done became apparent; *she had escaped*. Knowing her parents, they would have already started the hunt for her, but she couldn't, no she *wouldn't*, go back. There was no way she could live in that house another day knowing that her parents had plans to get rid of her.

Mentally shaking herself, Nicolette began to think of the best way to hide from her family. Staying in Boston was out of the question. There were too many people that knew her parents, and they would be all too glad to drag her back to that hellish place.

A sense of melancholy washed over her momentarily as she mulled over what she could have possibly done to make her parents hate her so much. With a shrug, she dismissed the nagging thoughts and began to focus on how she was going to stay out of her parents' hands.

Somewhere in the dark, a clock began to toll. It was 4:00 a.m. In 30 minutes the first train would be leaving the station, and she needed to be on it.

Drawing a deep breath, I centered myself and began to go through my options. As quickly as I considered a place, I dismissed it: Paris, London, New York, Washington,

D.C. I didn't have a passport and the other states were too close.

Slowly, I became aware of the footsteps of people making their way past me. I was running out of time. I needed to choose a destination right now!

Panic began to clog my throat, but then an idea popped into my head; the Amtrak. I needed to get to South Station. From there, I would have a pick of places at my fingertips.

Decision made, I slipped my feet into the pair of sneakers that I had grabbed on my way out the door but had completely forgotten were in my hands. With a nervous tug on my braids and a brush down my rumpled clothes, I joined the growing crowd of people heading into the station.

My eyes popped open and I jumped up looking around in alarm. For a second confusion clouded my mind as I tried to figure out where I was then in the next instance everything came flooding back. I was on a train trying to put as much distance as possible between my parents and me.

Now that I was fully awake, remnants of the nightmare floated through my mind. Upon reflection, it was mild compared to the reality. I sighed deeply as memories of that horrifying day came flooding back in vivid detail.

I was back in "that" room and "he" stood behind me smelling of leather, bleach, and a natural body musk that was none too pleasant. His scent would permanently be stamped into my brain. I could hear the scratching of his pen as he took notes of how I reacted to waking up to find myself strapped down to the bed. It was too familiar for me to respond, so I kept my eyes blank and my body malleable. It would make whatever he was going to do to me next hurt a degree less.

Of all the doctors I had seen over the last four years, he was the one that still sent my heart into overdrive and triggered panic attacks. His tests were borderline cruel, but my father said it was necessary, so I stopped asking for his visits to be canceled. It took a few minutes, but he finally stood in front of me. His steely eyes bore into mine, and he smiled curiously as he tightened the straps binding my hands.

"How are you doing today, my dear?" He was polite but disconnected. He could have

been asking about the weather. I ignored him and began my routine. Taking a deep breath, I slowly exhaled allowing my mind to delve deep into my subconscious. I was gearing up for the inevitable pain. Once I was deep enough, I would lose track of time and myself. It took a while, but after a half a dozen times I learned how to hide in my subconscious and re-live my happiest moments. Occasionally, but not too often and totally out of morbid curiosity, I would tune in to what the doctor was doing to me.

I was neck deep in my favorite memory when a phantom tingle snaked up my arms toward my face, twisting my body up and off the table. Another twinge moved through my body, and this time I felt more than just phantom pain; this bordered on the real thing.

The next wave got my full attention - it really hurt! The waves intensified even more until I was catapulted out of my subconsciousness and toward the forefront of my mind. A scream ripped from my throat as unimaginable pain tore through me. There was no relief: waves of agony, each more intense than the previous one, coursed through my body. I screamed and cried, hoping for a breather; praying for it to stop.

For something - anything - to happen, so long as I couldn't feel anymore. Still, it went on for what felt like hours until on the last spike my heart sputtered and stopped beating pulling me into the darkness of sweet rest. Just before I was totally swallowed by the blackness, I heard a loud bang. I saw the door fly open and my father stepped through with anger blazing in his eyes.

It was the only time my father ever apologized for the constant pricks and exams. He explained that I was one of a kind and that he and his friends had to study me so that they could keep me stable and healthy. I never did understand what he meant and threw a tantrum every time I had a visit. It wasn't until I met Dr. Titus Levi, the psychologists that I had begun to enjoy, somewhat, my yearly visits to the lab of hell.

Dr. Levi was a peculiar man. He was young, tall, had a square jaw, and was built like one of those old-time warriors you only see in history books. His eyes though, his eyes were my favorite feature. They were a weird moss green that I had never seen before and had a hypnotic quality to them. Every time he turned those peepers on me, I felt like he was seeing right through me and right into the depths of my soul. It was both unsettling and soothing at the same time.

"South Station! Please don't forget to take your belongings!" The blare of the T-worker's voice pulled me from my thoughts as the train slowed to a stop. I took another deep breath; I seemed to be doing that more and more lately, stood and did my best to blend into the crowd of people on their way to school and work.

Back at the Winspere's
That little bitch! "This is all your fault, Peter!" If you had just terminated the experiment when you first realized your hypothesis would not come to fruition, I wouldn't be walking around the neighborhood at 4:00 a.m. in the morning!"

"Shut up Sue-Ann!" "Maybe if you hadn't used her as your personal punching bag her whole life, she wouldn't feel the need to run away."

Peter and Sue-Ann Winspere glared at each other as they tried to figure out where the multi-million-dollar project could have possibly gone. It may have lived with them for the last seventeen years, but it wasn't their property, and if its rightful owners found out about this they would be screwed. With a roll of her eyes, Sue-Ann turned around and stomped towards the house.

"I'm not doing this shit anymore!" "She probably went to one of her little friends' house. She'll be back by tonight and when she returns you need to call Cassidy immediately and have them move up the termination order. I want her gone by the end of the night." With a curl of her lips, Sue-Ann walked off in a huff and left her husband of 19 years behind with a look of bewilderment on his face.

*****

Peter knew that his wife wasn't a devoted believer in the work that he and P.O.A.H (Protection Of All Humans) did, but he was genuinely taken aback at how dismissive she was of a child she had birthed, clothed, and fed for 17 years. He was not keen on the child either, but he had reservation about terminating her; after all, she was still a living being.

Hours had passed, and, there still was no sign of Nicolette. Even the school had called to inquire about her whereabouts. Sue-Ann was nonchalant about the whole situation but the later it got the more worried I became. *We had to find her!* Losing her was not an option.

It was 7:00 p.m. that night when I finally worked up the nerve to call to my boss. In less than 20 minutes the house was flooded with members from P.O.A.H who began a systematic search for their prototype. It only took the team 15 minutes to discover that Nicolette had gotten on a train to Chicago around 8 a.m. that morning.

Fear fluttered in the pit of my stomach as the news was delivered. This was beyond bad. Sue-Ann and I locked eyes, both of us thinking the same thing. We had two choices either we found Nicolette, and quickly, or face certain death at the hands of the organization.

Chapter 3

Free At Last. Right?

As I sat waiting for the Amtrak to leave the station a hundred different scenarios on how my parents would find me bounced around in my mind. It wasn't until I felt the first pull of the train as it left the station that I calmed down and my breathing returned to normal. *I was going to make it. I was going to be free!* With that thought, my anxiety melted and, in its place, a bubbling feeling of euphoria blossomed. *I was free! For the first time in my life I was totally free!* I threw my head back, and a carefree, genuine laughter spilled out of me.

"Excuse me, ma'am?" a soft brush to my shoulders sent a spike of fear down my spine, and I thought *"Oh no, they found me!"* I tensed, readying myself for a fight, but when I glanced up a pair of honey mint eyes met mine. I felt myself drowning in their depths and my next breath caught in my throat. Everything fell away for a few seconds as something in me recognized him. I was sure that I had never seen him before, yet I felt as though we were somehow connected.

He was tall, taller than my dad who stood at almost 6 feet high. His head of golden red hair almost touched the ceiling of the cabin. Tearing my eyes away from his I tried to focus on what he was saying, but the sound of his voice intensified the feeling of familiarity. My brain struggled to recover the memory of where we had met. I shook my head slightly and refocused on his words in time to hear him say "I believe you are in my seat."

"No, I don't think so; my ticket says 15B" I quickly searched my pocket and with a flourish, lips pursed, presented my ticket. With a raised eyebrow he took the ticket and read it over before a smile curled up against the edges of his perfectly shaped mouth.

"Actually, your ticket says Coach 15B; this is First Class."

"Oh, oh, I am so sorry, I didn't realize." Embarrassed and regretting the sass I had given him, I quickly gathered my things and made to leave the cabin. I should have known I was in the wrong place. Everything about it was too ritzy, for a $190 ticket. There was a sitting area and a door that opened into an area to lay down. It was fortunate that he had entered when he did because I was moments away from drifting off to sleep.

I was almost through the door when he called out to me, "Wait, you don't have to leave. It's a two-bed suite." As I glanced back at him a feeling of trust bloomed in my gut. *I was supposed to trust him!* I didn't know how but I knew that if I stayed with him, I would be safe. I paused for a few beats watching his eyes while deciding if I could rely on the sense of familiarity and safeness that the brush of his hand had instilled in me. Then with a slow nod, I sat across from him. "Can I just stay here like this? Won't I get in trouble?"

With a chuckle that reinforced my instinct to trust him and soothed my anxiety he shook his head, "They wouldn't even dare to open the door." I could have sworn that for a split second his eyes turned to red slits but when I blinked and looked at him again, they were back to honey mint. I leaned back and contemplated why I felt so at ease with him. The only other person that I had felt so at peace with was Dr. Levi.

"By the way, my name is Keith D'Vanni. If we are going to be sharing the suite manners dictate that I introduce myself." With a nod, I held out my hand "I'm Nikki." I still had a little reservation, and a lot of confusion, about how at ease I felt with him, so I wasn't quite ready to reveal my full name. "Thank you for allowing me to stay. You're not going to kidnap and keep me as a sex slave, are you?"

The cabin grew awkwardly quiet, but then he let out a burst of laughter that startled me. "You, little one, you are something else. My sex slave, huh? Well, I like grown women little one plus I am centuries too old for you." Shooting him a quizzical look at his odd phrasing I shrugged my shoulders "I just wanted to be sure. Anyway, just in case you get any ideas my parents are waiting for me in Chicago so they'll be looking for me if I disappear."

The moment I spoke the half-truth, Keith's grin slid off his face, and his nose twitched as if he was sniffing the air. "Hmm, really? Are you sure about that?" He asked as his eyes zeroed in on me. A sense of unease uncoiled and snaked through me when he spoke, and the temperature in the room seemed to drop a few degrees.

Averting my gaze, I bowed my head "Yes" and quickly changed the subject. "Do you live in Chicago?" When I didn't get an immediate response, I glanced back at Keith only to squirm in my seat as I met his questioning gaze. "You are an unusual one aren't you and you have no idea who or what I am?"

What he is?? I must be hearing things. "Are you a celebrity? My parents aren't big on television, so I have no idea who you are. I'm sorry if I offended you. If you'd like I can leave."

"No child. It's fine. Being around you is refreshing, he said with a grin on his face and a flash of mischief in his eyes. With that, the atmosphere around us lightened again.

"How about we raid the food cart? My treat." Before I could respond a voracious growl sounded from my stomach. Mortification rolled through me, and I hung my head in shame. I was so focused on getting away I had forgotten to eat. With another deep, rumbling, laugh Keith got up and extended his hand to me "come, let's eat."

I took his hand and with a wry smile followed him from the suite into the hallway. In just a few minutes, I was eating the best pasta primavera I had ever tasted in my life. I had been so engrossed in my food I didn't realize that Keith only had a glass in front of him until I was done. Wiping my face, I put down the knife & fork and looked across the table at Keith who was busy frowning into his glass.

"You weren't hungry?" I asked. He squinted up at me and I was shocked to see his eyes flash red again. This time I was sure I had not imagined it. He shook his head as if I had jolted him from deep thought and his eyes zeroed in on me as they had earlier.

Frowning and wiping my face again, I asked "Is there something on my face? Did I do something weird?"

Keith shook his head again, sat back in his chair, and sipped on a thick syrupy liquid. "You puzzle me is all little one. I am trying to understand who and what you are." His last sentence was quiet like he hadn't meant for me to hear.

"What I am? You mean a girl?" As if a cloud had cleared from his face, Keith suddenly smiled and chuckling he said "don't worry about it, my dear. Let's go back to the suite and see how we can entertain ourselves." Unfortunately for him, as soon as we got back to the suite and I sat down, I was out as quickly as if someone had flicked off a light. Exhaustion had finally caught up with me.

*****

I didn't quite know what to think of Nikki but I found her intriguing. At first, I thought she was one of those humans who followed me around in a desperate attempt to have me turn them. However, when she had looked up at me with eyes filled with apprehension and laced with annoyance, I immediately dismissed that assumption. She was a delight! Daring to give me attitude; something no one had done in centuries.

My interest had risen another notch when I moved further into the train cart and discovered she had a subtle yet distinct scent of my kind. She should have recognized me, but I sensed no change in her behavior towards me. As we spoke, it became clear that she was unaware of the existence of supernatural beings although she was connected to us, somehow.

I made a call as I watched her sleep. By the time we got to Chicago I would know everything there was to know about Nikki. If that was even her real name.

Chapter 4

A Little Bit of Karma

Within minutes of Nicolette being reported missing, the heads of P.O.A.H had called and demanded our presence at the home office in New York. There was to be a summit before the Council to find out how we could have possibly lost a multibillion-dollar piece of property.

Peter and I hardly had time to react before we were carted off to a private airport and onto a private jet. The moment we stepped onboard I knew that this plane was reserved for VIPs. It dripped with opulence. From the velvet seats to the minibar, to the young flight attendant who for a brief second, made me question my beauty, it was divine, delicious, and nothing short of exquisite.

It wasn't until the captain announced that we were about to land that I felt the first prick of fear. We would soon be walking into the lion's den, and I had no illusions; we had messed up on an immeasurable scale. Failed experiment or not, Nikki wasn't our property to lose.

The plane had barely touched down before we were whisked off and heavily armed security guards snatched Peter and me. Terror bubbled up from my stomach to my heart when they separated us taking Peter to the right and me to the left. I was quickly deposited into the backseat of a black, heavily tinted, Cadillac Escalade with men on either side of me.

By the time we pulled up in front of a nondescript high-rise building, my anguish had intensified. It jumped to new levels when the car doors opened and more guards appeared looking even more intimidating than the ones that had taken me off the plane. I was yanked from the car and hustled into an elevator that was as swanky as the private jet. My life flashed before my eyes, and I wondered if I would walk or be dragged out of this building in a body bag at the end of the proceedings.

When we stepped off the elevator there was a moment of silence before the hallway exploded into chatter. Shaking in fear, I suddenly found myself desperate to step back onto the lift. As though the guards could read my mind, they took hold of my arms and practically carried me to the front of the room. Peter was already at the defense' stand and I was stunned to see him sporting a black eye and bloody, swollen lips. Gazing into his eyes, I saw pain and absolute horror; he was petrified!

Having to defend ourselves in front of our boss and colleagues was my worst nightmare come to life. I had heard rumors about the four-seat Council. They only appeared once or twice a year, and that was only if there was a colossal scientific breakthrough or someone made an immense blunder and needed to be "handled."

For a second, a surge of anger washed over me. *All of this was all Peter's fault!* If only he had quit this job when he had a chance our family would not be in this mess. It's not like we needed the money. Not for the first time, I wished that the experiment they had inseminated in me had perished during the gestation period. My rage consumed me and I was lost in thoughts of how to put all the blame on Peter and extricate myself when cold, clammy, fingers touched mine

Peter was searching for my hand and once he found it, he interlaced our fingers. All the anger I was feeling towards him disappeared. The rage and fear was replaced by a sliver of warmth and the knowledge that no matter what we were about to face we would do it together.

A gavel banged suddenly, and the room quieted. My heart thumped, threatening to jump out of my chest. The trial of our lives was about to begin.

A monotonous voice addressed us breaking the silence. I gazed at the four councilmen searching for some compassion but all I saw was four white men that were indistinguishable from each other. They were pale, fat, and surprisingly, wearing a listless gaze that seemed to look beyond me.

Realizing that I was not going to get anywhere with them, I tuned back to the moderator, "...*Mr. and Mrs. Winspere, who have been brought before the council to clarify how they managed to lose one of this foundation's most sacred and priceless experiments.*" All the strength in my body seemed to drain away and I couldn't look up.

I could feel the judgmental stares of everyone in the room pressing in on me like tangible weights. I was too petrified to look, but I could feel Peter start to tremble.

One by one, testaments of our failure came to light. Men and women with whom we had worked for almost twenty years took perverse happiness in telling the council about our shortcomings.

I could hear the growing disbelief and anger in the voices of the council members each time a new witness took the stand. We had no chance of surviving this; there would be no redemption.

With tears streaming from my eyes I waited for the sentence to be handed down. Closing my eyes tightly I held my breath. There was a rustling behind the Council, and the crowd began to murmur. I peeked through my eyelids and to my surprise, and delight, Dr. Levi was whispering in the ear of one of the councilmen.

Hope surged through my body. Dr. Levi was always supportive of Peter and me. Maybe he would be the voice of reason that would stop this madness and save us.

I heaved a sigh of relief when the Council nodded in agreement to whatever was said, and Dr. Levi turned towards us. He was captivating to watch, like a dancer performing to a song only he could hear. Every move he made was precise.

As I watched, his eyes seemed to brighten until they were almost shining. Suddenly I was standing in the middle of my favorite fantasy. *I was in Bali, and the doctor was before me naked from the chest up. Up close, he was breathtaking - an Adonis come to life. Long-eyelashes closely cropped dark hair and delicate pink lips. Everything about him whispered of a sleepless night of ecstasy.* " Sue-Ann. May I call you Sue-Ann? You can call me Titus if it makes you more comfortable." His voice had dropped an octave becoming deep and hypnotic.

*****

Sue-Ann never stood a chance. Seduction was Titus' specialty, and he had been perfecting his skill for almost two millennia. He listened to her heart rate rise and the scent of her arousal met his nose. He grinned in satisfaction and delved right in. He fired a volley of questions at her. He asked about every nook and cranny of her life. No topic was off limits.

With a goofy smile pasted on her lips, a sordid story of hate and abuse poured from Sue-Ann. As the crowd listened to her, even the staunchest among them blanched in horror. By the time she was finished, Titus' eyes were switching from red to green until it settled on red slits. Icy fury unfurled deep inside him and spread throughout the room.

In an instance, the room erupted in chaos as Dr. Levi' features began to change. His irises bled into his pupils turning blood red while his skin turned deathly pale.

"YOU STUPID HUMAN! YOU DARED TO HURT MY CREATION!! WHO DO YOU THINK YOU ARE?! YOU PUNY TWIT."

Whirling to face the Council he growled his anger through clenched teeth, "and YOU, how could you allow a couple like this to take home my most prized possession?!"

Hell bent on vengeance, he moved towards the four men with a speed that defied logic. He grabbed the first one by the neck and twisted. A horror filled gasp echoed through the hall but no one moved.

He dispatched the second council member with the precision of a machine. Everyone was rooted to their spots watching in frightful curiosity.

Unlike the first two, the third councilman was prepared, and he tried to put up a fight, but Dr. Levi's movements defied both science and gravity. He sprung behind the councilman and plunged his claw into his chest ripping out his heart and watching it beat one last time. A strangled gurgle escaped the man's throat, and the light went out of his eyes.

The silence in the hall was deafening! The remaining councilman tried to run which seemed to amuse Dr. Levi because he allowed him to take a few steps before he pounced on his back. As they were falling to the ground, Dr. Levi grabbed one of his arms and ripped it out its socket. The sucking sound of the arm popping out of its cavity filled the room. Still, nobody moved! Then it hit me; *it wasn't that I didn't want to move it was that I couldn't move!*

Once the councilmen were dead, the doctor shifted back into his human form, stood up, smiled charmingly, and returned to the front of the room. There was a brief stillness, and then the moderator was handing down the sentence. Amazingly, we had been spared, for now.

*****

Peter and I would have to find Nicolette in order to redeem ourselves in the eyes of the Council. P.O.A.H would be sending someone else to look for her as well. If the agent found her first, we and everyone connected to us would be annihilated, but at least we had a chance to save ourselves.

I gazed at Peter and breathed a sigh of relief. No matter what, we had to find Nicolette, and we would start the second they released us from this hell hole.

P.O.A.H flew us home, but Peter and I were too preoccupied with figuring out the best way to save our lives to appreciate the luxury. When we arrived at the house, we barely had time to explain what was happening to the children before we were packed and on the next plane to Chicago. We tried to time it so we would arrive a few hours before Nicolette's train and intercept her at the station before she disappeared into the city making it harder to find her.

During the plane ride over my mind drifted back to the Council meeting but the only thing I could conjure up was a feeling of dread. Everything about it was hazy at best. I was just glad I walked away with my life.

Glancing over at Peter, I suddenly remembered how good it felt to hold his hand and sense his support. It was the first time in years that I had seen the man I had fallen head over heels in love with a lifetime ago.

As soon as we found the experiment and returned her to the Council, I would bring up the idea of a vacation. Maybe with a break from all the pressure we could get back to where we used to be before the abomination came into our lives.

Chapter 5

New Life

"Wake up little one. If you sleep any longer, you will miss the breakfast cart."

With a groan, I rolled onto my side and ignored Keith. The last two days had been filled with him hovering over me like a mother hen and questioning me about my parents at every turn. The latter I was able to avoid, but with the former, I had been less successful. Just as I was sinking back into unconsciousness, I felt a hard poke to my side that had me sitting up immediately in protest.

"Come on! I thought we discussed this; no poking at all it's too painful. Damn it, Keith! I'm probably going to be sore all day."

Popping an eye open, I glared at the mischievous grin he was sending my way. For a moment a murderous rage enveloped me, and in my mind's eye, I saw myself putting my fist through his chest. A giddy feeling spread through me at the prospect of his blood spilling and with it an urge to drink it.

Horrified at the thoughts and urges running through me I quickly stood up and shook my head but not before I caught the satisfied smile that flashed across Keith's face.

It was gone in the next instance replaced by concern at the perplexed look on my face. "Are you okay, little one?" I nodded my head and headed to the corner we had designated as our changing area. With a rustle and slight murmur, of "see you at breakfast" Keith left me to myself.

It wasn't long before I joined Keith at breakfast and shortly after the conductor announced that we would be arriving in Chicago soon.

A bout of anxiety flooded my system as I thought about my next move. It was weird, but after the first night with Keith, I felt as though he had been coaching me on how to live off the grid.

He had talked about when he was younger and fleeing from his responsibilities. He had gotten a lot of fake papers so that his parents wouldn't be able to find him. He even told me the name of the guy he used and how much a fair price would be.

When he first spoke about it, I had been terrified, thinking that he had caught on to what I was doing. After a few minutes, I was thankful to see that he was just reminiscing. *Getting to know each other,* he had said. After the initial fear had worn off, I had become annoyed at his constant yammering, but I listened to every word.

Before I knew it, I was packing, and the train was coming to a stop. I had decided on my way to Chicago that I couldn't stay there. It really was not that far from Boston, and because I used my ID to purchase my ticket, I would be easily tracked.

The moment I got off the train, my instincts kicked in and something whispered that I should hide behind Keith.

Without hesitation, I stepped behind him as we exited and narrowly missed the gaze of my parents who I spotted just as I left the last step.

Fear ran through me as I realized how right Keith had been. My parents had tracked me her and if I hadn't moved quickly, I would have gotten caught and dragged back to hell.

Keith suddenly turned to look at me. He must have seen the terror in my wide eyes because he shrugged out of his jacket. "Put this on." He draped his coat over my head and pulled me under his arm; blocking me from sight. We walked a few feet before I heard Keith murmur something to someone and I was tossed inside of a car.

The car door clicked closed and I dragged the coat off. I glanced around and was bewildered to see that I was sitting in a limousine with a woman and a man who looked just as startled to see me.

A few awkward beats of silence passed before Keith cleared his throat, "Now, Ms. Nicolette Winspere, would you like to explain to me why you are running away from your parents?"

Blinded by fear I dove for the door handle; ready to jump out at the sound of my full name. I barely moved before I was roughly tugged back down into my seat. It happened so quickly that for a second, I doubted that I just tried to leave.

Tears began streaming down my face. I looked at Keith, hesitantly. He looked slightly annoyed and hurt by my actions. "I have known who you are since the first night, Nicolette. If I wanted to do you harm or turn you over to your parents I would have already; don't you think?"

I became more anxious as I realized just how terrifying this man was. "Who are you? And why are you helping me?" There was silence in the car as the other two passengers pretended that I wasn't there while Keith leveled a piercing gaze at me.

"It doesn't matter little one. What matters is that I would like to help you. Of course, you would owe me a favor."

I stiffened at his words, "Help me how and what favor?" Keith nodded at the couple across from us, and a manila-envelope appeared from nowhere and was placed in my hands.

"Here is everything you need to start a new life. A birth certificate, driver's license, passport, and other papers that will back up the story that you are Nikki Hall. A 20-year-old graduate from Amherst with an English degree."

My mouth popped open but I was speechless. *Who the hell was this guy, for real?!* Not only did he know who I was and about my family, but he had also created a fake identity for me. "I-I, what do you want from me?!" I yelled out in an octave so high it rattled my own eardrums.

Keith raised an eyebrow and leaned forward with a look of disapproval. "I just need you to answer a question for me. After that, Damien here will take you to the airport where there is a ticket to Phoenix, Arizona waiting for you. You will never hear from me again. In fact, you will forget we even met."

I watched him carefully waiting to feel that prick in my heart that usually told me if someone was lying or not but there was nothing. If anything, everything in me was telling me to trust him which made me even more perplexed.

I opened the envelope and saw the documents Keith had promised. *This was crazy! I was crazy!* I was also desperate, and these papers were exactly what I needed to get away from my parents for good. With an almost imperceptible nod, I agreed.

"Good! Now I have a few questions, and you must answer truthfully. If you don't, I will know and will make sure you find yourself back in the clutches of your parents."

I blanched but nodded again; this time vigorously.

"What are you little one? Vampire or werewolf?" For a moment I was silent thinking that he was joking but as the seconds ticked by, and I saw the sober look in his eyes, I realized that he was dead serious. I glanced over at the couple across from me, wanting to see if they were just as stunned as I was at Keith's stupid question, only to see creatures from horror stories come to life. Their eyes had turned into red slits and their incisors, no those were fangs, were bared and resting on their bottom lips.

"What the fuck?! What the hell are you guys?!" As quickly as I could, I scrambled into the corner pressing myself into the door desperate to get away.

"*NICOLETTE ANSWER THE QUESTION!*" Stuttering in fear, I turned to gesture at Keith about the freaky shit happening across from me only to find that he looked exactly like them.

My heartbeat accelerated, and my eyes widened to the point of being painful as I stared into the eyes of death.

"I, I, oh my God, please let me out! I don't taste good I promise! Oh God! You have to let me go I promise I won't tell anyone. Just don't kill me. Please, oh God please!" I had become a blubbering fool; begging for my life while I tried to think of a way to get out of my current predicament.

With a growl, that had me screaming, Keith was suddenly right over me. "I already told you that I would let you go if you told me what you are!"

Cringing in terror at his sudden change in appearance, I covered my face but couldn't stop myself from responding, "W-w-what I am? Human? I'm human! I promise I-I've never seen your kind before."

My hands were grabbed by what felt like iron shackles that lowered them to my side. "Say it again and look directly in my eyes as you say it," The moment that I felt him grab my hands I lost control of everything and a wet stream ran down the side of my leg, I looked into the eyes of certain death and spoke. "I am human."

*****

"Okay, little one. Here is the airport." I blinked and blinked again feeling like I was waking up from a nap I didn't remember taking. A memory tickled at the back of my mind, but I came up blank. All I remember was Keith saving me from the sudden appearance of my parents at the train station and giving me free papers to start a new life.

Chapter 6

Five Years of Change

"Unexpected but it's true
The feeling's old and yet so new
Swept away in just a few lines
against all odds and all the signs
Is this a dream?
pinch me please
I could scream
With such an ease
I could smile
With just a word
I could fly
like a bird
Unexpected
but it's true
The dream is real
and so are
You"
by Afrodita Nestor

Those eyes, those red- slit-like eyes, drew
closer mouthing something I couldn't quite
hear but what was clear was the murderous
intent streaming from them. Fear and a
desperate need to escape crawled through
me and I was forced up and out of my
subconscious with a piercing scream.

I popped up with my heart hammering and fear still clogging my throat. I opened my eyes to reassure myself that I was alone in my room only to slam them shut. The small beam of light streaming through the left of my lilac blackout curtains was excruciatingly bright.

Allowing a few beats to pass and my heart rate to slow, I opened my eyes once again. This time the light didn't bother me anymore.

I sighed in relief but also in exasperation at the shitty way my morning was starting. I closed my eyes again and counted backward from ten.

As I recounted, the vividness of the dream swirled through my mind reminding me that it was five years to the day since I had escaped the lab of hell.

On this day every year, no matter where I was or who I was with, I would be haunted by those murderous eyes. I had never seen anything like them before not in movies, not in person, and certainly not the day that Keith had graciously rescued me. Yet year after year something deep within me whispered that they were real.

Lost in thought, I absentmindedly glanced over at the clock on my dresser. "Crap, Crap, Crap" I was going to be late for yet another doctor's appointment. Flipping back my maroon silk sheets I slid from my bed and sped to the bathroom. There was no way I was going to see my favorite doctor without taking a shower first.

Six minutes later I was stepping out the fastest shower of my life and starting my hair routine. It was always the same. I would spritz water over my hair followed by moisturizer, then coconut oil, then castor oil, and finally two big braids down the sides that met in the back to form a bun. It was simple cute and easy to do.

As soon as I got to Phoenix five years ago, I had decided to wear my natural hair. While my hair had thrived, growing healthy and thick, it took a lot of time and effort to get it into a manageable style.

Rushing out of the bathroom, I quickly applied lotion to my skin. I threw on the first pieces of clothing I put my hands on, a pair of dark, loose-fitting jeans and a pink blouse. Then I sprinted out the door.

Thankfully my doctor was only fifteen minutes away, and the traffic wasn't bad today. I was only five minutes late. As I drove up to the nondescript white building, I psyched myself up. Everything was going to be solved today. All the episodes of overwhelming noise, insatiable hunger, and sensitivity to light would be explained, and I'd get the necessary medication and be back to normal soon.

I found a parking spot and power walked to the building with hope dogging my every step. For a slight beat, I felt an odd yet strangely familiar sensation of an intense stare. There were hundreds of people mulling around, but no one was looking directly at me, so I quickly shook it off and decided that I was just paranoid.

I was almost at the check-in desk when I faltered perturbed to see that Cassy was the receptionist on duty.

Something about her made my skin crawl. She looked ordinary enough with blue eyes, waist-length dark hair, and a petite frame but it was the way she stared at me. She eyed me like I was the answer to all her questions. It reminded me of the lab of hell, but I comforted myself with the thought that there was no way anyone from my old life could have found me. As always, I dismissed my feelings, but it didn't stop the shudder that flowed through me when our eyes connected.

"Good Morning Cassy. I'm running a little late for my appointment with Dr. Carol." With a sickly-sweet smile and that look in her eyes, Cassy buzzed me in. "Not to worry Ms. Hall. She's waiting for you. Just go to Room 2. Oh, by the way, I heard that your test results came in. Hopefully, everything is fine." For a brief second, there seemed to be a flash of malicious triumph in her eyes, but it was extinguished as quickly as it appeared.

Sending her a perplexed look I nodded, "Um, thanks." With an awkward wave and a wan smile, I walked through the door. *What the hell was that all about?* Anyway, I was way too happy about getting a diagnosis to give her words much thought.

I was hardly in the room before Dr. Carol Bishop walked in behind me with a somber look on her face. She looked like how I pictured my grandmother would if she were still alive. Warm dark chocolate eyes, a portly body, and brown sugar colored skin that aged with the grace that spoke of royal ancestry.

"Take a seat child. I have news, and I'm afraid that it is not good. Your blood test came back inconclusive." Holding her hand up to stem my questions, she continued… "Based on the symptoms you described, I went ahead and sent your samples to a colleague of mine who studies rare genetic diseases.

She was flabbergasted by the results. What she found was that on a molecular level, all the cells in your body are breaking down and being replaced by new ones so dense that even with her most powerful microscope she couldn't see pass the outer membrane. I'm sorry child, but you seem to be morphing into a being neither she nor I have ever seen before." She is so intrigued by the results that she sent me a request to meet you.

Dr. Bishop went on to explain a few more things, but I was lost in a daze. Nothing she said made any sense. *Cells breaking down? Changing into something unknown?!*

I watched her mouth move, but the words fell on deaf ears. I was busy trying to stop the growing sense of dread that arose in me from sweeping me away like a bug caught in a tsunami. *I have to get out of here!* "I have to go, I can't…" Stumbling to my feet, I yanked the door open ignoring Dr. Bishop' calls and dashed toward the front door intent on breathing fresh air.

I was caught in an unreal state. Everything around me was muted and moving in slow motion. The air seemed to hum and the feeling that someone was watching me returned.

I was almost to the door when I bumped into a hard body and lost my footing. Big, warm, hands grabbed and steadied me but didn't let go. For a moment I wanted to stay in those arms and ignore the world. Cursing at my weakness, I glanced up to say thank you and was sucked into the cat-colored orange eyes of a man I thought I would never see again.

Detective Josiah Walker of the Boston Police Department: Missing Persons Unit was standing before me. From the look of regret and longing in his eyes, this was not an accidental meeting. I didn't care why he was here. I would never trust him or anything he had to say ever again.

He was the last person I wanted to see, especially after the news I had just received. Wrenching myself out of his hands, I slid by him and was gone before he could react.

*****

Three years ago

"Hi, I'm Josiah." I couldn't believe it! The hot guy with the British accent that Tianna and I had been perving on for the last ten minutes while waiting in line for a cashier was speaking to us! We were at the Dunkin' Donuts around the corner from our jobs and since he had entered every female in the vicinity had tried to get his attention.

Between his dark coffee colored skin, caramel light eyes, dimpled smile, full lips, and muscled body, he was enthralling. At first, I thought he was going after Tianna. Even though she was married, guys often hit on her. After all, she was the prettier of the two of us. Long hair and big brown doe eyes had always made her a favorite amongst the opposite sex. Surprisingly, after a few minutes of mundane chatter, he asked for my number and wanted to know if he could see me later that night.

Although I was twenty-one, it was my first
date, and he had made it incredible. We
went to dinner and spent the evening
laughing and talking about everything.

He had asked a lot of questions, and at one
point I felt a bud of unease in my stomach,
but I brushed it aside since he was so
forthcoming with details about his own life.
After that night, we only saw each other a
few more times, but we texted and called
daily.

It occurred to me once that I had no idea
how old he was or even what he did for
work. As much as we talked, he never
brought up either topic, and I never bothered
to ask. I just knew that he held my attention
and I felt safe when he was around. I didn't
suspect anything until I saw him on the
television about a month after we met.

I was flicking through channels searching
for something to watch when his familiar
face flashed across the screen. I flipped back
to the channel excitedly only to have my
worst nightmare come to life.

There he was; standing at a podium next to a
man I could only assume was a police
Captain. He was dressed in a dark formal

jacket with silver buttons over a white collared shirt with a black tie, pleated pants, and white gloves. The caption on the bottom read, "Detective Walker awarded the Police Lifesaving Medal for tracking down a kidnapping victim who had been missing for two years."

I freaked out! Now I knew why he had never mentioned his job. He was working with my parents to retrieve me! There could be no other explanation. I felt betrayed and stupid, but underneath those feelings was an underlying rage. We might not have been a couple or even dating officially, but he had lied to me.

To make matters worse, when I Googled him, I found out that his job was to work closely with families to find and bring home missing kids. He was known for being relentless in his search and had a high success rate.

I was on the phone with Tianna trying to explain to her, through my tears, that I had to leave town when there was a knock at the door. A wave of fear crashed over me making me dizzy. My parents were here to take me! Josiah must have told them where I lived. Croaking a goodbye to Tianna, I sprinted towards the back door praying I could escape.

I was almost through the door when I heard his booming voice. "Nikki! I know you're here. Let me in. I can explain." There was a pause, and then I heard a desperate plea; "Please." I wavered although I knew that I should run. My parents would kill me if they got their hands on me, but I had built a life here, and I didn't want to leave.

I ambled to the front door and paused contemplating my options before fumbling with the locks. Gingerly opening the door just enough to see out. I looked past him expecting to see my parents. "Please Nik; I just want to explain; I would never do anything to hurt you." *"You already have"*, I thought, but I opened the door fully. His head was bowed and when he looked up his face was twisted with guilt and shame. "May I come in? I can explain. Please". I watched him carefully, searching for a sign that would give away the real reason for his visit…to turn me over to my parents.

I couldn't discern anything other than regret, so I moved aside and let him in then stepped out for a moment to look up and down the hallway making sure there was no one else

around. "It's just me, Nikki. I promise."
Hearing the word "promise," I snorted.

As if that was supposed to mean something to me! I listened intently for a few seconds while watching for any movement before stepping back into my apartment and closing the door quickly. Fastening all three locks, I stepped back and checked to make sure they were all latched securely. I wasn't taking any chances! If he had brought my parents, it would take them a few minutes to get through that door giving me time to escape through the back.

Taking a deep breath, I turned toward Josiah and just looked at him. Three days ago, we had been curled up on the sofa watching "The Escape Plan," but right now, I didn't want to be within one foot of him.

The fact that my parents had convinced him to help them find me meant they must have told him some made up, horrible, heart-wrenching story. Although that's not something, they would have done on their own. One of my teachers or friends must have realized that I was gone and forced them to file a missing person's report.

Josiah watched me as I watched him. My mind was a whirlwind of questions, but the loudest one was how much of the last month was true? "Nikki," he began... He paused to search my face, but it was blank. He ran his hand over his face, a nervous tic I had become familiar with over the last month. He took a step closer to me, but I stepped back. "Don't! Just tell me why you are here and then leave."

Hurt clouded his face for a moment. Then he nodded and began to speak. "Your parents didn't hire me, not directly. On average, two thousand kids are reported missing every day. As one of the best trackers in the department, I get to choose which cases I will take. I always follow my gut when choosing. The moment I saw your face something tugged at me, and I took your case."

He had stopped to look at me again, probably to try to read my face, but I had learned a long time ago how to control my facial expressions so that I showed no emotions. I could tell he was debating with himself. Several times he looked as if he was going to say something or reach out to touch me but thought better of it.

"I approached your family, not the other way around. According to the case file, they believed someone had come in and kidnapped you in the middle of the night while they slept. The officers who got assigned to the case noted that there were some discrepancies in their report, but they could not prove it. By the time I got your file, you had been missing for about a year and were at the legal age to be on your own but because your disappearance was reported as a kidnapping it was still in our database.

My job isn't necessarily to bring kids back to their parents. It's to find an answer and close the case. I searched for months but there was no trace of you in Phoenix, so I put your file in the cold cases archive. Finding you was a complete fluke.

A few months ago, I had a rough case involving a girl who had been missing for five years. Her captor had kept her alive but when he realized I was closing in the bastard killed her. To be that close and lose her...I wasn't the same after.

My Captain forced me to take a few weeks off. When I ran into you at Dunkin 'Donuts, I was shocked. Instead of investigating you,

I decided to get to know you, Nikki." I
blinked, and suddenly he was in front of me,
holding my hands. He had moved so quickly
I had no time to stop him or step away. He
towered over me, using his height to his
advantage as he stared down into my eyes. I
couldn't deny the passion between us. I had
begun to fall for him. "I'm falling in love
with you, Nikki."

I froze, my chaotic thoughts coming to a
dead stop at his words. H-he was falling for
me?! With a roar, my mind retaliated. *Like
hell!*

Wrenching myself from his grasp, I shouted,
"No! You don't get to say that! You don't get
to have feelings. You lied to me. You could
have just told me what you did for a living.
You could have told me that my family
asked you to look for me, but you weren't
really on the case. Now you want me to take
your word for it?! Josiah, I can't."

I shook my head vehemently, "There is just
no way! I would always be wondering if you
are lying to me or if you will change your
mind one day and rat me out to my parents.
I'm sorry, Josiah, but I can't."

I could only imagine what I had looked like, my eyes wide with fear and disbelief as tears leaked from them. I don't remember much more about that evening. I do recall that I woke up the next morning on the couch, wrapped in a blanket. That was the last time I had seen Josiah Walker.

*****

"Nikki" My name like a caress came from behind me but I ignored him and quickened my footsteps.

I was steps away from my car when those warm hands from earlier clasped my elbow and pulled me into an embrace. I almost released the torrent of tears that had been building since Dr. Carol gave me my test results.

I soaked in his warmth for a couple of seconds choosing to forget just how much of a liar he was while I got my emotions under control. With a shuddering breath I pulled away without turning around, "NO! Just no. Not today Josiah. I just can't."

My voice sounded pitiful and small even to my ears, but with a sigh and a kiss to the back of my head he released me. My knees went weak and for a slight second I wanted to turn around but I forced myself to jump into my Volkswagen and speed away.

Chapter 7

Is Change Good?

With my heart hammering in my ears and my thoughts a jumbled mess, I drove towards home. I needed to be surrounded by the familiar sweet scent of vanilla and cinnamon; lay in the plushy goodness of my futon sofa, and binge on lots of ice cream and cake until today's events were lost in a haze of sugar. After I came down from my sugar rush, I would open a bottle of wine and slowly process just what had transpired.

I was a street away from home when my phone began to ring. "Let It Flow" by Toni Braxton sounded and without looking I knew it was Tianna.

Tianna Moran was my only friend who knew a little about my crazy past. She was grace personified and looked like she had stepped out of a beauty magazine. Being around her always filled me with confidence and power. She was in a word intoxicating and how she juggled a husband and a six-month-old baby while holding down a job as an executive at a large firm, baffled me.

Her life was perfect unlike mine that was filled with unexplained issues; mostly medical ones that got worse with each passing year. I felt a faint prick of jealousy and rolled my eyes at myself. She was exactly who I needed to talk to.

I hit the answer button. "Hey T." My voice wobbled both from stress and relief.

A hoarse whisper came through the line, "I need you to come over." Her words sent the strangest sensation of dread down my spine and the pity party I was having came to an immediate end.

"Come over? Are you sure?" For as long as I had known Tianna, I had never been to her house not for a party, a sleepover, or even to pick her up.

"Yes please and hurry." The tremor and urgency in her voice had me swallowing my questions and stepping on the gas pedal.

"Okay. What is your address? I'll be there before you know it." Tianna stuttered her address through sniffles and before I could respond the gruff sound of a masculine voice sounded and the line went dead.

The test results from my doctor's appointment and running into Det. Walker became distant memories as I sped down I-

95. My heart was in my throat and the dread I felt earlier settled in the pit of my stomach.

The GPS said forty-five minutes, but barely twenty-five minutes later I was pulling into the Moran's driveway. As I walked up the steps to the door, I noticed how isolated their house was and that it was eerily quiet.

It was one of those huge, old, colonial homes with a massive back yard. There was the main house and another much smaller one for the help. In my mind, I could practically see my ancestors picking cotton in the field.

I shrugged my shoulder dismissively, rang the bell, and waited for Tianna. A minute passed with no answer. In fact, there was no movement at all on the other side of the door. Frowning in concern, I rang the bell again then double checked to make sure that one of the cars in the driveway was hers.

Still, there was no answer and the awful feeling I had on the drive over was now in full bloom. Grabbing my cell, I dialed her number but it rang without an answer. I couldn't even hear it through the thickness of the door.

Something within me awakened and the most peculiar sensation of pins and needles spread through my body, and suddenly I could see every dust particle in the air and hear the woodpecker in the tree about two feet to my left and 8 feet off the ground. I could even smell the mulch that was piled in the backyard.

Before I could panic at the abrupt influx of heightened senses, a muffled sound of skin connecting with skin followed by a voice pleading for it to stop flowed to my ear.

I immediately recognized Tianna's high-pitched voice as well as the angry, growling voice of her husband, Michael. From the sound of things, he was smacking her around.

Rage erupted like a bubbling cauldron that had been waiting for the perfect moment to explode and all the anger I had been suppressing came rushing to the surface. In a moment of delirious animosity, I braced my hands against the thick wooden door and gave it a brutal shove.

Like butter giving way to a knife, the door exploded inwards. Without giving it much thought, I stepped through the arch dismissing the modern day décor that radiated wealth and impeccable taste. Pausing for a moment, I cocked my head to the side, tapped into my acute hearing and sped towards the sound of Tianna's distressed whimpering.

In a blink, I found myself in the master bedroom which made mine look like a storage room. I was in awe of the gold paneled windows, the Borchers upholstered panel bed, and a low hanging chandelier that sparkled and shone, that was until I saw the scene playing out in front of me.

All two hundred and fifty pounds of Michael Moran was delivering deadly kick after kick on a tiny silk-robed figure curled into a ball, Tianna.

My fury rose to epic proportions and before I could think I was yanking Michael by his arm. In my madness, I spun him around, grabbed his throat, and released a fiendish growl. The gagging sound of his choked breathing fueled the urge to spill his blood. I wanted to see his body ripped and mangled until he was nothing but I messy pile of bones and blood before me.

"N-Nik," the low moan from Tianna snapped me back to reality and the impulse drained away.

Stupefied at my actions and thoughts, I quickly dropped Michael and reeled backward with horror in my eyes. *What did I just do? How did I...* "Nikki, help me."

Whirling around I looked at Tianna who was attempting to sit up but failing. Her pretty cocoa skin was black and blue and wrapped in her arms was little Aria.

I hurried over to help her. I was at a loss for words partly because I was stunned at my actions and partially in shock at the state she was in. Taking a sleeping Aria from her, I practically carried her on my back out of the house.

The drive home was a blur, and before I knew it, I was pulling into my assigned parking space. The car was silent except for the occasional sniffle from Tianna. I was bewildered at how this day had turned out. It was not at all like I planned it in any way, shape, or form.

I didn't know what to say. *What could I say?!* Releasing the breath, I hadn't realized I was holding, I opened my door and walked around to Tianna's side. I opened the door and pulled her out of the car into a hug.

As if a dam inside of her had broken, she burst into wails that made my heart tighten. After ten minutes of her crying out the anger and pain, I gently stepped back and retrieved my god-daughter from her hands. Not a word was spoken between us as we headed to my apartment. We were both lost in thoughts of what had transpired in the last few hours.

There was something seriously wrong with me! Maybe the doctor wasn't as crazy as I thought. I was changing and becoming someone, no something, that neither my medical team nor I recognized.

The unexplained strength and the overpowering compulsion to rip into Michael today were just more symptoms I had no idea how to handle. With a sigh, I entered my apartment.

While Tianna attended to Aria, I spent the next few minutes cleaning up and resisting the impulse to bury my sorrow in multiple bottles of wine.

*****

Today went as well as I expected. I was annoyed and frustrated at Nikki's rejection, but it didn't matter; I had to talk to her. I had spent the last three years, in the shadows, protecting her from P.O.A.H and her parents but that was about to end. There had been an increase in chatter about her case. It looks like P.O.A.H had hired someone else to find her and this person was a ghost. There was no name, no trace, nothing I could find out about him or her. All I knew was that they had located Nikki and had even made contact.

I had no choice but to warn her. She was, after all, my mate and there was no way I would allow such an organization to get their filthy hands on her. All these years later, I still had no idea why they wanted her so badly.

I growled in frustration as I watched her through the window. I was too far away to protect her adequately.

Chapter 8

What Choice?

Like the flicker of a TV channel, I went from relaxing in a bed of tulips, orchids and chrysanthemums to being surrounded by darkness. Thrown off by the sudden change, it took a moment for my mind to catch up and another for fear to slither up my spine making the next breath desert my body.

As a little girl, I hated the dark, but it had become a full-blown phobia after that errant memory from five years ago. Caught in what was quickly becoming an anxiety attack, I almost missed the squeaking of a door opening and the quiet footsteps that followed.

I glanced up hoping Tianna had come to my aid. I stiffened in trepidation as those same predatory eyes with blood red, slit-like, pupils from five years ago walked towards me. "No, no, no this can't be happening" bounced around my mind.

Sheer terror wrapped around my limbs like a vine leaving me glued to the bed. My eyes widened tearfully and my heart galloped a hundred beats a second while my breathing became shallower and shallower. I was sure I was about to die until something within me awakened and that peculiar sensation of pins and needles started running through me again. Waves of strength and determination crashed through my body and I instinctively knew that I could demolish anything in my way.

With that knowledge came a savage impulse to conquer everything in my path. Zeroing in on the eyes in front of me, I allowed my instincts to take over while I waited for the steps to get close enough for me to pounce. Just a few more steps and all of this would be over. I would finally know…

*****

There was a thud as I landed face first on the floor. Tears sprung to my eyes; *I had been so close!* Pushing myself up into a sitting position, I rubbed my smarting nose as I tried to recall the dream.

Suddenly, like a flash flood rising from nowhere, the sound in my room jumped to what sounded like a billion decibels almost blowing out my eardrums. *It was happening again!* I could hear everything! The chime on the door of the bakery a few doors down from my apartment, the frightened yell of a mother telling a child to hold onto her hand, and the click, click, click of the traffic light as it changed colors. It was as if I was standing outside instead of safely ensconced in my apartment.

The noise increased with every passing second until I was weeping for relief. Clasping my hands over my ears, I rolled around the wooden floor, scraping my skin, as the pain reached an impossible crescendo. With a piercing scream, I collapsed and sank into the blissful quiet of darkness.

The next time I opened my eyes everything was back to normal, thankfully. As I shifted a bit, I realized that I was no longer on my bedroom floor instead the familiar earthy brown of my living room walls surrounded me. Someone had laid me on the couch.

Glancing around, I was thrilled to see Aria to my right. She was snoring quietly in a makeshift bed on the love seat. A smile drifted across my face at the peaceful smile on hers. Then, I remembered what happened earlier and I was reminded that whatever was happening to me was accelerating. I needed help and there were only two people I knew who could even remotely help me. I had been thinking about it since I got home last night but I tried to bury it deep in my mind. Unbidden, a memory floated to the forefront of my mind.

The steely eyed doctor had once again used the hateful syringe that made my breathing painful. Somehow, I fought through the pain and ran off when he wasn't looking.

I hid in the janitor's closet for hours before my father found me. The look of fear in his eyes scared me as he grabbed and shook me silly. "You can't run off Nicolette! Not now, not ever! You are one of a kind and we don't understand much about your body, yet. Without us, you could get sick and die. Do you understand? No more hiding or running away!"

As it turns out, he was right. Five years later, I find myself having no choice but to go home and hope that whatever was wrong with me hadn't reach a point of irreversibility.

For a brief moment, my mind railed against going back to my parents; but what choice did I have? A few more episodes like the one earlier and my eardrums will really be blown out. I needed their help and hopefully enough time had passed that they wouldn't still be pissed off at me.

With my mind made up, I sat up and called out to Tianna. Heated whispers followed before Tianna answered, "In the kitchen." A frown marred my face as I walked towards the kitchen and the source of the whispers. As soon as I walked in, I wished I hadn't. Standing across from Tianna, looking like he just walked off of an ebony magazine set was the man I had blown off yesterday, Josiah.

"I-What are you doing here, Siah?! And why did you let him in?!" As frustrated and angry as I was at the sight before me I couldn't summon enough energy to put much emotion in my voice.

"I didn't let him in. I wouldn't!" T swore vehemently shooting Josiah a disdainful look. "He just burst through the door when you started screaming."

Josiah straightened up and strode towards me a look of concern and desire swirling in his eyes, "She is telling the truth. She didn't let me in. In fact, she has tried her best to get me to leave for the last hour; but I refused. Not until I saw for myself that you are awake and okay."

Nodding in understanding, I backed up a few steps refusing to let him crowd or touch me. "Okay." I gestured to myself, "I am fine, thank you for stopping by, please leave." I knew I was being a bitch but the intense look in his eyes was triggering a well of feelings, I didn't want, in the pit of my stomach. Averting my eyes, I stepped to the side and pointed at the door.

"I can't. We need to talk." He had barely uttered the words before I was shaking my head. There was just no way. Not only did I not want to talk to him, I didn't have the time.

"There can't possibly be anything that we need to talk about. I think you said everything you needed to, three years ago.

And this is honestly the worst time for you to want to rehash things. I have a lot of problems I need to deal with."

In the blink of an eye, he was standing in front of me. His cat-colored orange eyes stared down into mine tugging free all the emotions I had been trying press down and I started to cry. "I know, love" his voice had roughened, and he tugged me into a hug.

The seal broke and I wrapped my hands around his waist and cried. I had missed him! The pleasant spicy smell of him that was mixed with tangerines. Most of all, I missed the strength that filled me every time he was around.

I don't know how much time passed but I was finally able to think clearly so I pulled out of his embrace and looked down. I caught the flash of hurt in his eyes at my actions but I needed to put some distance between us.

I was getting ready to ask him to leave again when he spoke, "I know about the unexplained changes you've been experiencing lately." Silence followed as I whipped my head up and stared at him in shock.

"What did you just say? H-How do you know about that?!" Alarmed at the revelation, I took a step back only for him to re-close the gap, boxing me in between the fridge and his towering body of steel. Dismay coursed through me. "No, no! I said NO!" With a powerful surge, I pushed him back and ran towards Tianna.

Putting myself between them, I glared at him as my suspicions began to rise. "How do you know about me, better yet, how do you even know where I live?!"

As I watched, his eyes began to glow and dissolve into slits just like the ones in my nightmares. Unease rippled through me prodding something deep within to respond. Out of nowhere, a growl erupted in the room causing the hairs on my arms to stand up. I was poised to run, and drag Tianna with me, at the inhuman sound so Josiah's nod of approval almost went unnoticed.

"That's exactly what I thought," he said, stopping me in my tracks. "You're human but you are also a werewolf."

That was when I figured it out. *That growl had come from me!*

Chapter 9

I Have To Go Back

"What the hell are you talking about?!" Fear ran rampant through my body even as something within me simultaneously rebelled and relaxed when he said werewolf. Not another word, I didn't want to hear another word. "SHUT UP AND GET OUT!! "GET OUT!"

I was trembling in fear and something else I refused to acknowledge. "Nikki, we have to talk! You are part werewolf and I know how it happened."

Shaking my head in denial I pointed at the door; Get the F-OUT NOW!!"

"Can you stop being so stubborn-" The growl from before ripped through me again and the now familiar feeling of pins and needles started to sweep over me.

Josiah threw his hands up in surrender, swallowed his male pride, and backed away. "Okay, Okay. When you are ready to talk give me call. Here is my number." With a flick of the wrist he threw a card on the table and turned to walk out. "You are in a lot of danger, love. I just want to keep you safe."

"I can take care of myself, Josiah. I don't need you. Not now, not ever!"

As soon as I heard the front door close all the strength in my body drained away and I sagged down. Tianna was barely able to catch me, before I hit the floor, and help me into a chair.

"Nikki, Nikki! Are you okay? What was that!?" *That was a good question. What was that?* I didn't miss the fear in her voice or the way she kept darting looks at my throat trying to figure out if she had really heard me growl like an animal. I remained quiet. I had no answer for her.

"What was Josiah talking about?" With a ragged sigh, I looked up at my friend and shook my head. "I don't know, and I don't care. You know, as well as I do, that he can't be trusted. A werewolf…really? What am I, a character in a sci-fi novel?!"

I tried to put her mind at ease, but the fact is I _had_ just growled like a damn character in a sci-fi novel. *This was getting out of hand!* I drew a quick breath and squelched down the growing fear in my stomach. I looked over at T and tried to decide if I should tell her what the doctor told me yesterday.

Tianna seemed to sense my reluctance to say anything else because she suddenly wrapped herself around me in a fierce hug. "I don't care what you are Nicolette. I just care that you are safe and healthy." It was exactly what I needed to hear.

With a wry smile, I tried to figure out where to begin, "It isn't good T. Something is happening to me, and the doctors have no idea what it is."

"What do you mean they don't know what it is? They are doctors, right? What did the tests show?" The aggrieved look on her face was a well needed balm for my soul.

Watching her face, I continued "The tests were all inconclusive. My red blood cells are dying and being replaced by mutated ones that are so dense, not even the strongest microscope can see beyond the surface. There is something seriously wrong with me, and I think the only people who can help me are my parents."

She exploded into a hot molten pot of fury, "Are you crazy?!! No! You can't go to them! Did you forget what they did to you as a child?! Oh. My. Goodness, Nikki! No, just NO! You just can't; those people are insane oh-"

"I know T, I know, but that's exactly why I have to go home. They knew what was going to happen to me. That was probably what all those tests were about." I sent her a pleading look even as she shook her head in anger and disbelief.

"There has to be a different way Nikki, you can't go home to those monsters." Throwing my head back, I let out a haggard laugh.

"Do you think I want to go back into the damn dungeon of hell?! I don't have a choice. I need help! You saw what happened yesterday and just now. It's been going on for a while and has been getting a whole lot worse lately. I'm at my wits end T. I need my parents."

An intense silence descended on the kitchen as we stared at each other. Aria had woken up in all the commotion and suddenly let out a squeal of delight as she tugged on her mother's shiny, dangling, earring. Not even her usually infectious laughter could lighten the mood. My eyes pleaded with Tianna as she leveled a "no way look" at me. Finally, she blinked, heaved a sigh, and nodded.

"Fine but I'm coming too. There is no way I'm allowing you to go back to Boston without backup."

Josiah gnashed his teeth as he stood in the hallway listening to the discussion happening on the other side of the door. Since the day the P.O.A.H group had hired him to find Nicolette nothing had gone as planned.

His record had been spotless before Nikki. He always recovered his targets using everything at his disposal including his cover job as a detective. Right from the start he knew this case was different. It was the first time the target was a teenage girl and also the first time they wanted a live recovery.

As soon as he saw her picture his whole world spun on its axis. The alpha wolf in him that had been dormant for so long sprung awake. Nicolette Winspere was his mate! *How could that be when is she human?!*

When he had caught up with her in Chicago, five years ago, he had despaired about letting her escape without painting a target on his back.

It was a pure stroke of luck that she was in the company of Keith D'Vanni, a member of the royal vampire race.

It had given him a legitimate reason to allow her to escape. It had hurt; allowing his mate to get away but it was for the best. At least she would be safe. What he hadn't counted on was meeting her again in Phoenix.

It was entirely accidental, and following the draw of the mate-bond, he couldn't resist introducing himself and then spending time with her. It nearly broke him when she found out about his job as a detective and cut him out of her life, but he knew it was necessary for her safety.

Somehow it didn't work and P.O.A.H had found her. They were doing everything they could to force her into their hands and she was falling into their trap.

Something wasn't right! The organization was too desperate to get her, and he had no idea why. Worse, there was something going on with Nikki.

When he first met her, and during their later encounters, her scent had been a mixture of human, an occasional whiff of werewolf, and a sickly-sweet smell. He had always brushed it off; figuring that someone in her life was a werewolf. But yesterday and today he realized just how wrong he was.

The scent had been coming from her all along. She seemed to be transforming into a werewolf which should have been impossible. The creation of werewolves was strictly forbidden and anyway she smelled like a natural wolf not an infected one. Nothing was adding up which meant only one thing, he had to go to P.O.A.H headquarters to find out what was going on. After he saw her off to Boston, that was.

With a heavy heart he walked away from her door and to his car where he called in a favor so he could track her credit card for any airline purchases.

*****

"Are you sure about this Nikki?" Tianna asked for the hundredth time. Annoyance swirled through me, but it was tempered by my own uncertainty.

I wasn't sure going to Boston was really a good idea but what could I do. "No T, but what choice do I have?" Heaving another sigh, my millionth of the day, I sunk completely into the first-class seat and closed my eyes. We had managed to get a red-eye flight from Phoenix to Boston. It was a 5 ½ hour flight and I needed to rest if I was going to deal with my parents.

As I was sinking into the blissful release of sleep, I had the same question that had swirled around my mind all day. *Was going to Boston a wise choice?*

*****

Grey eyes watched with bated excitement as the plane took off for Boston. A manicured finger pressed a key and the phone dialed a preprogrammed number.

The call connected but no one spoke, "She is on the way." The call immediately disconnected and a few seconds later beeped with an incoming message. "Booked on the next flight. It's time."

A wide smile spread across thin lips. She had searched for years for the failed experiment, and now she would be able to eliminate the threat that was Nicolette Winspere.

Chapter 10

I Walked Into Hell

Aria's weak cry pulled me awake. My eyes flew open and I quickly snatched my goddaughter from the hands of her snoring mother. Glancing out the window, I was surprised to see the familiar gas tank near Logan airport. We would be landing in Boston in just a few minutes.

That explained why Aria was fussy. Her ears were probably popping from all the pressure. Rocking her back and forth proved to be soothing for both of us and I lost myself in playing peek-a-boo and listening to her cute giggles. Before I knew it, the wheels touched down and immediately a feeling of foreboding surged over me.

I was willingly stepping back into the lion's den and I had no idea if I would be able to escape again. I looked over at Tianna who was still snoring. She must be exhausted after the last few days. Running my hands down her shoulder I gently shook her awake.

I slapped myself, mentally, as I realized that I had yet to ask her if she was injured or even if she needed to go to the hospital to be checked out.

"T, T, are you okay? I've been so selfishly concerned about myself I forgot to ask you how you're doing."

Chuckling at my guilty expression, Tianna's eyes roved over me and her baby before leaning forward and kissing Aria on the forehead.

"Only you would feel guilty about taking care of yourself first and I am fine, trust me. This is not the first time…"

The look of despair on my face reminded her that I wasn't privy to the intimate details of her life.

Tianna blew out a gust of air and stopped herself from continuing. "Let's wait until we are checked into the hotel to talk about this."

Nodding my head in a daze at her words, I almost missed when the seat belt sign went off indicating that it was time to deplane.

We made short business of retrieving our things and getting out of the airport. Throughout the whole process I couldn't shake the nagging feeling that I was being watched.

Shaking my head, I chalked my paranoia up to being in Boston again and quickly ordered a car from one of the ride sharing apps.

It was a twenty-minute drive from the airport to the hotel in downtown Boston and I spent the entire ride stiff as a board while memories of my former life bombarded me.

For the first time in years, my siblings ran across my mind. *I wonder how they turned out.* The youngest and I were six years apart, making her roughly fifteen years old, so she should still be living at home. I had missed five years of their life. I wonder if they still hated me and how they would feel about me coming back…

With a small groan, I shook those thoughts out of my head. It didn't matter. I needed my parents and convincing them to help me was my biggest worry. The relationship between my siblings and I could wait.

Some Time Later

As soon as Tianna and I got to the hotel we had a long discussion about her home life and I let her in on the rest of the horrific details of my past. It was liberating to finally share everything about myself with someone.

For Tianna, sharing her story was cathartic. I had never seen her cry so much as the sordid details of her marriage came pouring out. There were instances that I felt like she was still hiding some things from me but I nodded and hugged her regardless.

My friend had endured a lot and I had no right to judge her. All that mattered is that she wanted a change and as soon as my parents fixed whatever was wrong with me, I would help her divorce that ass and get her settled somewhere far away from all the drama.

When we were finished, we settled in to eat brunch and I reached for my laptop. Before leaving Arizona yesterday, I had tracked down my parents' email and sent them a message. After all this time, they still worked at the largest genetics lab in Boston.

I waited to check for a response until now. Partially because I was on a plane but mostly because I was scared that they hadn't replied or worse they had replied and told me to drop dead.

*****

It had been five hard years since that little bitch had run away. Five years since the organization was so far up our asses we couldn't fart without it being recorded. Everything we did was monitored.

The only thing I was grateful for was that they had spared our lives. Somehow Peter and I had missed Nicolette in Chicago but were lucky and whoever they sent to retrieve her had failed too. That had earned us a conditional reprieve.

The reprieve itself was a joke. Once a year they would haul us in front of the council to explain to them what was being done to find their precious experiment. It was humiliating to have to re-hash our failure year after year. Even worse, our co-workers had taken to avoiding us so they wouldn't be associated with the team that had failed so miserably.

Over the years we had searched for Nicolette becoming more desperate each time we had been hauled to New York to report that we had yet to find her. Then today, today, all my prayers had been answered. Out of the blue, I received an email from Nikki asking if she could come home because something was wrong with her.

Pure happiness had exploded through me. I had been so excited that I rushed to Peter's office, interrupted his meeting, and quickly ushered everyone out.

As soon as the room was empty, I jumped on him and attacked him with kisses. Before I could explain why I was so happy our kisses became passionate and my lab coat was on the floor followed by the rest of my clothes soon after.

It had been a while since that type of passion had erupted between us. Following Nicolette's escape, I had been able to control or dissuade Pete's advances.

As soon as we were finished, I laughed. Apparently, Nikki had been good for one thing. She had gotten me the best lay I'd had in a very long time.

"Peter, Nikki sent me an email! Something is happening to her and she's coming back to Boston for our help. We are going to be free my love! Free from the organization. We will finally be able to escape their grasps."

Peter smiled and after another mind-blowing round of sex, we sent an email to the organization and waited for them to tell us how to proceed.

******

Nicolette's nerves were threatening to drive her mad. The relationship between her and her parents had never been good yet here she was at a restaurant anxiously waiting to meet with them.

She had been beside herself that morning. Wanting to show them just how sophisticated and elegant she had become, she had hogged the bathroom and done a complete beauty routine.

She started with a face mask then plucked her eyebrows and her chin. The biggest struggle was her hair. Afraid that her parents would disapprove of her natural curls, she considered straightening it.

Thankfully, she caught herself just in time. Her hair was a part of the woman she was today. She loved how it coiled and curled to her head after a shower and the natural volume it had even after it was combed out. She was proud of her hair and there was no way she would change it to please anyone.

She eventually settled on chiney bumps in the front and a poofball in the back and finished with a light slather of edge control. When she finally emerged from the bathroom she looked like a Nubian princess.

As good as she looked, it still wasn't enough to stop the constant spikes of fear and uncertainty in her tummy. She was fidgety and jumped every time the doors to the restaurant opened.

"For the love of heaven Nik, stop that! You are making me freak out." Tianna interrupted her reverie. "They apologized in the email didn't they? Plus it sounds like they want to make amends and help you so stop freaking out. Besides that's why I am here. If they try any funny business I will knock them out."

The goofy grin on my best friend's face made me burst out laughing. She couldn't hurt a fly but knew the promise would help calm my nerves.

Lost in a battle of wits, neither one of us noticed my parents entering until I was suddenly engulfed by a lady in a cream-colored trench coat.

*****

The look of dubious shock on Nikki's face was all I needed to confirm that this was in fact her mother.

"Nicolette, oh my goodness; Nicolette, we've missed you so much. I was a horrible mother to you. I am so sorry!" Mrs. Winspere' sharp wail was shocking. She sounded nothing like the cold woman Nikki had described to me.

Soon after, there was a gruff voice behind her; "hey, hey, stop hogging her. I want to hug her too." It was a tall man a little smaller in comparison to my husband's 6'2 but no less imposing. He moved in and wiggled his way in between the mother daughter duo.

Nikki's eyes connected with mine. Bewilderment and happiness glowed in hers and a few tears escaped down her cheek. I couldn't imagine what such a reaction from her parents meant to her. Suddenly, I felt my wet cheeks and realized that I was crying too. I truly hoped that their reaction was the start of beautiful relationship between the three of them.

Chapter 11

I'm in the Fire

Everything happened so quickly that it left my mind spinning. The man and woman I remembered from my childhood had transformed. My mother looked the same. She hadn't aged a bit in the past five years, but the shame, guilt, and a little bit of hope that rolled across her face invariably were new. I had never seen her express those emotions before, much less towards me.

Unexpectedly, she was even giving me an explanation for her behavior back then. Apparently, she had been suffering from mental issues but was now on a slew of medication that stabilized her moods, so she wasn't so cruel anymore.

My father sat next to me rubbing circles into my hand and throwing in a bit of apology here and there as well. I was genuinely floored but before I could sufficiently process anything, I could feel one of my episodes coming on. The noise level in the restaurant was rising, and my mind was zeroing in on the conversations around me.

"I-I, I'm sorry, but I have to go. I can't."
Sending a panicked look to Tianna and
gesturing to my ears I quickly got up almost
falling out of my seat as I scrambled to get
to the bathroom. I prayed that putting a solid
wall and a door between me and the
thunderous noise would make it diminish.

As I rushed off, I glimpsed the shocked look
on my parents' faces at my sudden departure
but I desperately needed to get away. I
barely made it inside the bathroom before
everything reached a crescendo and I all but
collapsed inside a stall.

*****

"Mr. and Mrs. Winspere, you have to help
her! I'm Tianna by the way. Sorry I didn't
introduce myself before. There is something
you must know about why Nikki came back
so suddenly. Lately, she's been having
these…episodes. Sometimes it's her hearing.
It will magnify to the point where she can
hear everything within a five-block radius
and then she passes out. Then there are
times when her eyes will be so sensitive to
light that she draws her curtains and can't
leave her darkened room for days. Other
times she'll be extremely ravenous but
eating makes her sick.

I was able to convince her to see a team of doctors back home but they were useless. Every test they ran on her came back showing either inconclusive or that she's okay.

There was even one doctor who suggested that the episodes were in her mind and that she should seek professional help for it. That doctor I gave a piece of my mind, but I digress.

The point is that Nikki needs your help right now. She's having one of those episodes, and that's why she ran off to the bathroom."

The crying, concerned, couple who had only seconds before looked bewildered, and a little hurt were now looking at each other with such calculating eyes that I was stunned. It was like watching a mask fall off. Almost immediately, the look was gone, and I doubted what I had seen.

"She has progressed that far? We need to get her back to the lab right now. Tianna, is it? Come, help me carry Nikki to our car. My love, settle the bill and start making arrangements."

Mrs. Winspere was quick on her feet firing commands and rushing towards the bathroom. She tried to look concerned, but this time I saw it. There was a veiled look of perverse pleasure in her eyes. Something wasn't quite right.

There was nothing I could do though. I had promised Nikki that I would give her parents the benefit of the doubt because they were the best genetic scientists on the East Coast. Still, I didn't trust them; not for a moment.

New York

Josiah was sitting in front of a P.O.A.H computer hacking into their database. He had flown to New York late last night with the intent to find out what made Nikki so crucial to the organization. What he found had floored him.

Nikki wasn't human at all! In fact, she was a biogenetically engineered vampire-werewolf hybrid that had been implanted into Sue-Ann Winspere. If he hadn't seen the numerous case files of past and ongoing experiments with his own eyes, he wouldn't have believed it; but here it was, all laid out for him.

It didn't make any sense though. Yeah, there were several humans, mostly scientists, who knew about the supernatural race but there was no way they knew enough to make a successful clone much less to create one from scratch.

Something was wrong! No human could run this company successfully. It had to be a supernatural, and if he was right, it was a vampire.

During his last meeting with the four seated councilmen, he had noticed some odd behavior. It was only now that he was looking at the information in front of him that he figured it out.

The men were under a powerful mezmur. A mezmur was when a vampire would essentially hypnotize other beings and turn them into puppets. Very few vampires could do this, and if memory served him right, only the oldest of old had truly mastered it.

He had to find out who was behind this. With a quick click, he copied all the files to a thumb drive and continued searching through the mainframe computer. There was something that had been bothering him about P.O.A.H for a while now. Who was the owner?

As he dug deeper, there was a sudden, quick, flicker of light. The computer's camera had been activated! Josiah swore, swiftly detached the thumb drive, and scuttled out the room.

His digging seemed to have tripped some type of alarm. Whoever was behind P.O.A.H did not want to be found. Chances are he had just painted a giant target on his back.

*****

Moss-colored eyes gleamed in the dark as it stared at the photo of the young wolf who had often been used to get rid of his enemies. It seemed that he had slipped up somewhere and now he was being investigated. It didn't matter though; his treasure was almost in his grasp. As for Josiah Walker, his usefulness had come to an end.

*****

When we found Nikki, she was in the stall unconscious. Mrs. Winspere and I managed to get her in the elevator and into their car with little commotion.

I hopped into the car and could tell that Mr. Winspere wanted to stop me but his wife gave an almost imperceptible shake of her head and he stepped on the gas.

Luckily, or so they claimed, we were close to their lab. Within minutes we were able to get her inside and plugged up to so many machines that my head spun.

While medicine was not my forte, there were a few instruments that I recognized, and thankfully the rest didn't look as though they were too dangerous.

In a flash, Mr. Winspere, who I hadn't even realized had left the room, re-appeared over Nikki and stuck her with a giant needle.

"Hey-" just as I was about to voice my alarm Nikki came to with a cough. A look of panic flared in her eyes when she saw her father over her. I quickly hurried over and held her hand. "Hey sweetie, I'm here."

With an audible sigh, she calmed down and sat up. "I'm sorry about breakfast. I have been having-" "Don't worry I already explained it to them." I interrupted and squeezed her hand in reassurance.

"Yes, Tianna has explained everything. She is a good friend. I am glad you found someone to be there for you when we couldn't be."

Mrs. Winspere' eyes glistened, but I wasn't buying it. Just a few seconds before Nikki woke up; she had shot me a look filled with contempt and annoyance.

Mr. Winspere jumped in, "but, we are here now and will take care of you."

I wasn't surprised. Something told me that they would eventually try to get rid of me, so I was prepared. I jumped in before Nikki could say anything that would jeopardize her parents' willingness to help.

"I know we have just met Mr. and Mrs. Winspere and you don't know anything about me, but I have been by Nikki's sides for the last five years and I know *everything* about her. I can't, in good conscious leave now in her hour of need. I have to stay and support her."

There was a tense silence as Nikki's parents communicated with just their eyes. Nikki looked at them pleadingly while holding my hands in a death grip.

After a few more seconds passed, they nodded, and Mrs. Winspere replied, "you are right my dear, and you have been a good friend indeed.

Since you are here, why don't you help us get Nikki situated? We need to take several blood samples and run a battery of tests. We will know in a few hours just how dire her condition is."

I nodded graciously and said thanks but not before shooting her a triumphant look. They may have fooled Nikki, but I saw through their act although I just couldn't understand why they were behaving like this.

Even as I sent her that look, I knew they would try another way to get Nikki by herself. A few hours had passed, and slowly the results of the tests began to come back.

At first, they had been excited but as the day wore on and the rest of the test results came in the happiness that had been pouring from them earlier vanished.

Although I was talking to Nikki about trivial things to distract her from the constant probes and prick, I was paying close attention to her parents so I didn't miss when Mr. Winspere stepped into the corner and made a phone call.

For the first time since entering the lab, the haughty look he had been wearing disappeared, and he looked anxious.

Whoever he was talking to seem to scare him shitless. His lips hardly moved and I realized that whoever was on the other side of the phone was either someone he had a healthy dose of fear of or his boss.

The conversation didn't last more than a few minutes but his dark skin glistened with sweat by the time he hung up. On unsteady legs, he walked over to his wife and whispered something in her ear.

She blanched and looked over at Nikki and then at me. She gave Nikki a blazing look of scorn mixed with triumph but the moment her gaze shifted to me she assumed a sad, lost look.

I could tell that they had figured out how to get me away from Nikki and the theatrics were about to begin. However, since Nikki had rescued me from my husband, Michael, and taken me out of that house, I had found my courage again. She had saved me, and my baby's lives, so I refuse to allow her to be dragged into whatever scheme her parents were concocting.

Chapter 12

The Trap Closes

I watched with apprehension as Mrs. Winspere approached Nicolette, her eyes glistening once again. "Nikki, oh my dear, I wish I had good news, but your father and I are at a loss. Your tests results are beyond us. We have come up with a way to stabilize your remaining cells and make them harder to die, but, they will die my dear.

We shouldn't give up hope though. There is a doctor who specializes in rare genetic diseases. She is the best of the best. Your dad had a brilliant idea, so he made a phone call just a bit ago hoping to talk her into seeing you. Unfortunately, she is retired and can no longer do house calls.

You will have to go to her, and it has to be at night. She suffers from a rare disease called Xeroderma. It doesn't allow her to go out during the day."

Everything Mrs. Winspere said sounded reasonable. There was just one problem: the glint of unnatural gleefulness deep in her eyes. I had a feeling that where ever she was sending Nikki it wasn't some reclusive doctor but somewhere far more dangerous.

"Okay, how soon can I see her?" Before I could voice my concerns, Nikki was nodding in agreement with her mom.

Grinding my teeth to stop from blowing up I pasted a smile on my face and hugged Nikki in celebration just as her mother came over with a relieved look on her face.

"This is for the best Nicolette. The serum that we developed…we can't say how long it will last and don't want to give you any false hope. Dr. Wilson is the best person for the job."

I was extremely grateful when they gave Nikki a case of the serum they had developed and told us to wait for their call. I felt as though we were escaping the lion's den.

I tried hard to convince Nikki to take a rideshare back to the hotel, but I was shot down by the happy family of three who wanted to spend more time together.

Looking at Nikki's glowing, cheerful, face I knew I couldn't make too much fuss; not without coming off as an outsider who was stopping a happy family reunion.

I was patient the whole ride listening and even joining in on the jokes and reminiscing but the moment they dropped us off my smile dropped as well.

I was about to go into a rant about how fake her parents were, but as I looked at the waves of happiness floating off Nikki, I decided to wait and talk to her about my suspicions tomorrow.

*****

I was screwed! Ever since I had breached the security at P.O.A.H headquarters, I was being followed. There was no doubt about it, there was someone else running P.O.A.H, and I had gotten onto their radar.

I was in the middle of buying a ticket to Boston when my private work phone went off. There was a new target available on the dark net. I typed in my password and froze when my face popped up.

I was toast! There was a $2 million dollar bounty on my head. Swearing up a storm, I logged out of my account and went into clean-up mode.

I always knew this day could come. With several quick keystrokes, I systematically began destroying everything that made me Josiah Walker. It had been ten years since I assumed that identity and although I had become attached to it because it brought me, my mate, I had no choice but to get rid of it.

Within five minutes all electronic traces of Josiah Walker disappeared, and all apartments linked to him went up in flames both literally and figuratively.

I stood in front of my New York apartment and took a second to say goodbye to the last ten years of my life. Just as I was about to get into my car, the glint of a sniper rifle scope shone off the side mirror. I dove for cover, and a mere second later a high caliber bullet whizzed by and shattered the glass exactly where my head was a few seconds ago.

I swore out loud and quickly rolled under my car. I always parked over a manhole. It was a filthy escape route but one of the best.

I was halfway down the steps when I heard the sound of a Glock being cocked and fired. There was a painful burning in my arm followed by one in my shoulder and then my chest.

Uttering another flurry of swear words, I managed to pull out my own gun and shoot off a few rounds. I heard the satisfying splash of my attacker hitting the sewage and exhaling a dying breath before I sunk into unconsciousness.

*****

Three days had passed, and I was no closer to dissuading Nikki from going off with her parents to see this Doctor Wilson.

In fact, we had barely spent any time together. Every day either her mother or her father made sure they joined us for breakfast, lunch, and dinner. Yesterday she hadn't come back to the hotel until late into the night sending me into a near panic.

We had gotten into a shouting match which resulted in Aria waking up crying. That worked like a bucket of ice cold water being dumped on us. I had quickly calmed down and told her of my suspicions. At first, she had staunchly defended her parents, but after a few more minutes of talking she had broken down in tears.

"I know something isn't right T, but what can I do? They are the only hope I have left. Whatever serum they gave me has stopped the episodes and I feel more like myself than I have in a long time.

I am just as apprehensive as you are, but I have no choice so please just support me and hope for the best."

I nodded grudgingly. I understood, better than most, her need to see the best in a crappy situation. I also knew that things were not going to work out how she wanted, but she was right. She had no choice but to trust her parents.

For the first time since arriving in Boston, Nikki told her parents that she was going to take me sightseeing and spend some time with her goddaughter.

The next day I fell in love with Boston. Between the walk through the Commons where the flowers were in full bloom, the mini-concerts in the square s by Macy's, and the bustle of Haymarket with its exotic smell of spice and food, I was at peace in a way I hadn't been in a long time.

When we finally got back to the hotel it was late and hunger was clawing up our insides, but still, we were laughing and joking.

Then suddenly Nik's cell phone rang. The sharp sound scaring us so badly I almost dropped Aria who shrieked and clutched my arm.

"Don't answer it. We are about to eat. We have to be able to stuff our faces without your parents for one night" I said rolling my eyes and sneering at the shrilling device.

With a shake of her head and pleading in her eyes, Nikki answered the phone and instantly paled. It wasn't just her parents calling to nag her. Dr. Wilson was ready for her.

Tears filled my eyes as I tried to open my mouth and beg her not to go. I just knew, somehow, that I would never see her again. However, this was life or death for Nikki so kept my mouth shut.

I hugged Nicolette and watched her get into the back of her parent's BMW. There was a giant knot in my stomach and I prayed that this was not the end.

Chapter 13

Caught

"She promised! Damn it! She promised!"
That was all I could think as I watched the
morning sun rise through the hotel window.
It was close to eight hours and I had yet to
hear anything from Nikki although she
promised to call me as soon as she arrived at
Dr. Wilson's. Worse, her and her parents'
numbers kept going to voicemail. As hours
dragged by, the fear in my heart grew until I
couldn't draw a full breath.

Poor Aria, my little boobie was feeding off
my crappy energy and had been fussy since
waking up. I bobbed her up and down in my
hands as I paced the length of the living
room hardly noticing the room décor that
had only days before left me in awe. I was at
a loss! *What could I do?* I had no idea where
Nikki was or how to get a hold of her.

As the fear in my heart grew so did my
desperation. At the edge of a mental break
down, I contemplated doing the one thing
Nikki had expressly forbade me to do…call
Josiah.

Nikki would probably skin me alive when
she found out, but at least she would be in

front of me and not missing. I drew in a ragged breathe and raced to my room.

While I balanced Aria on my hip, I turned my bag upside down and searched through it for the card Josiah had given to Nikki. She had tossed it in the trash but I had retrieved it when she wasn't looking. I knew that there would be a day that we would need his help I just didn't think it would be this soon.

Taking a deep, calming, breathe I punched in Josiah's number and prayed that he would answer. One ring, then two, by the fourth ring I was ready to hang up, dreadfully disappointed, when the line suddenly connected.

"Hello, Josiah, is that you?" There was a brief pause before a hypnotic voice answered, "Josiah is out of communication at the moment darling. I'll have him call you back when he's well." My heart skipped a beat, there was something sensual about this man. I could sense it even through the phone.

"I can't wait. Tell him it's about Nikki." There was another pause, this one filled with reluctance, followed by footsteps and the man's voice.

"Hey, mutt! Wake up! There is someone on the phone saying it's an emergency involving Nikki.

There was a painful gasp and a groan before the rustle of the phone exchanging hands and then Josiah's hoarse voice crowed in my ear. "Nikki?!"

"No, it's Tianna but Nikki is in trouble and I don't know what to do." As the words fell from my lips all my pent-up frustration and fear also fell as tears from my eyes.

"Shit, shit! Tell me exactly what happened."

It took almost ten minutes, but I spilled everything that happened since Nik kicked him out four mornings ago. When I was finished there was a deafening silence on the other end followed by a crash.

"Josiah, Josiah?"

There was a flurry of swearing so colorful I was shocked and impressed at the same time. Just as I was going to call out for him again, footsteps sounded followed by growling and hissing that sent unease down my spine and plugged my throat with trepidation instead of words.

"Keith, you have to help her. It's Nikki! The girl you helped to hide from her parents 5 years ago and said you have been watching over ever since." There was another long pause and the voice that answered the phone was on again demanding my location. I stammered it out through the fear that gripped my heart at the cold fury that now filled the voice, a stark difference from the sexy voice that had answered.

"I'll be there within the hour," forgetting that he couldn't see me I nodded "and Tianna," "Yes?" "You need to leave that hotel right now. Chances are if Nikki's family has kidnapped her you will be at the top of the list of people they want to get rid of so they can cover up what they did."

There was click and in the ensuing silence my blood ran cold as I processed what the voice had said. A few heartbeats later I was a tornado. I tore through the room grabbing all of Aria's things and a few of my own.

I was halfway through packing when a thought occurred to me, *I couldn't walk out the hotel with my luggage. For all I know Nikki's parents has someone watching the place. I would have to be slick about leaving; but where would I go?*

The anxiety in the pit of my stomach was rising again. Just as it was about to flood my throat my cellphone beeped scaring me so badly I almost let out a scream.

I picked up the phone and was surprised to see a text from an unknown number. It was an address with a message below it. *"Go here until I arrive. You will be safe. Leave everything. There will be clothes for you and the necessary items for your daughter."*

The tension in my body slipped away and I almost burst into tears of gratefulness. Whoever Josiah was sending was a godsend.

Within 5 minutes, I packed Aria's small baby bag and walked out the hotel. I had intended to call a taxi but with danger breathing down my neck I thought it best to take the bus first and then jump into a cab.

*****

My parent's silver BMW was moving quickly down the highway making good time to the outskirts of Boston. We had been talking about my life back in Phoenix when out of nowhere we were surrounded my four black Hummers with dark tinted windows.

At first I wasn't worried thinking that they were with my parents but then I noticed the shocked look and unease in my dad's eyes and the tightening of his grip on the steering wheel. They weren't with us. Something wasn't right. I was about to call out to him when all the cars stopped short. It was so sudden that my father had no time to maneuver the sedan and even if he did, there was nowhere to turn.

Brakes screeched and there was a thwack as we crashed into the car in front of us. None of us were wearing seatbelts. Just as the force of the crash propelled me forward, I moved instinctively, and at lightning speed, grabbing my seat belt and wrapping it around my arms so I wouldn't be thrown out the car.

It was just in the nick of time and instead of my whole body flying through the windshield, my head smashed into the center console and I blacked out.

*****

The throbbing in my head was the first thing I felt. Groaning in pain, I tried to open my eyes only to be met with a blinding light that sent my ears ringing. Intuitively, I tried to raise my hand to cover my eyes only to realize that I couldn't. There was something wrapped around my hand. Wiggling a bit more I came to the horrific realization that

all my limbs were bound. *I was trapped!*
Someone had strapped me to a table.

I am back in the library of hell! With that
thought, I let out a bloodcurdling scream
that reverberated through the room.

"SHUT HER UP!" A terrifying and familiar
voice rang through the room scaring me into
immediate silence. With a herculean effort, I
snapped my eyes open only to be sucked
into the moss-colored eyes of Dr. Levi Titus.

"D-D-Dr. Titus?!" At that moment, the pain
in my head reached new excruciating
heights and I was sucked back into the dark
abyss of unconsciousness.

Chapter 14

This is the End

The next time I opened my eyes the bright lights were all gone. In fact, everything was dark. Moving my hand, I was disappointed to find that I was still strapped to a table. There was an eerie silence surrounding me and with it the intense scent of someone I hadn't seen in a long time, Dr. Levi.

I was confused and perplexed. Of all the people I expected to see, he was not one. His presence didn't make any sense. Had he rescued me after the accident and if so, why did he have me strapped to the table? "I know you are there."

For a beat there was nothing and then from my left a harsh manic laugh floated through the room as the piercing white lights came back on.

For a moment my eyes burned and teared but I blinked through it determined to see his face. Instead I was overcome with dismay to see that I really was back in the lab of hell. The same sad grey walls, big windows so that I could be observed and that damn door red door that was the start of all my nightmares in this place.

Lost in my growing despair I had almost forgotten that Dr. Levi was there until he spoke, "I knew it! You are so close my dear I can smell them."

Smell them?! I parroted in my head as one of the only men I had admired and looked up to during the worse times of my life came into my line of sight. When I had seen him earlier I thought it was a trick of the light but seeing him now I confirmed that I wasn't hallucinating.

He hadn't aged a bit! He had to be at least my father's age but he looked as vibrant and young as the day I first met him. The white, cotton, dress shirt he was wearing paired with the casual black slacks only increased his youthful aura.

His gaze locked with mine. His eyes blazed with a frenzied glow that made me think that he wasn't all together there.

"Doctor Levi," I began as I searched for the right words to say that would get me out of this situation.

"Doctor Levi, I-- help me please."

The slow grin that spread across his face in response was more horrific than the laugh he had let loose moments ago. In that instance,

I knew that there was no escape for me. I had fallen into the hands of the devil.

With a speed that defied logic, he was suddenly straddling me and caressing my face. Revulsion mingled with panic swirled through me and I began to struggle involuntarily. I had to get out of these restraints.

"None of that my dear. You asked me to help you and that's exactly what I intend to do."

With a playful wink, he leapt to the ground and disappeared leaving me bewildered and in a pool of my own sweat.

"Oh my...what the hell is going on?!"

"Do you know how old I am little girl?" The stentorian voice of the doctor appeared out of nowhere. Causing a new coat of cold sweat to break out on my skin as I swiveled my head from left to right in a frantic effort to pinpoint the direction of his voice. There was a small breeze to my left and a blur flashed by me causing an unintentional flinch.

"Well do you?!" his voice sounded again and this time the breeze was to my right. I swore I saw a white lab coat. Confusion slowly gave way to disbelief as my *other* senses kicked into high gear allowing my mind to slow down the blur and the doctor's face became clear.

"Good! Even without you trying your abilities are breaking through. You saw me just now didn't you?" This time his voice came from above and I shrieked when I realized that he was crouched right over me again.

My mind balked at his sudden appearance and I tried desperately to scooch away from him; even as the bindings dug into my wrists and ankles. "Answer me Nicolette. Did you see me?" His voice boomed through the room scaring my nasolacrimal duct into production.

Tears and mucus streamed down my face as I stuttered a response "I-I-yes, I saw you. Do you know what's happening to me?"

"But of course my dear! After all I created you.

Created me?! What?!

"Hmmm…you aren't progressing fast enough. At this point, all the artificial human DNA should have already been replaced." The doctor had continued on dismissing my clear shock and dubiety. The more he spoke the more I was left speechless.

"Dante!" There was a small scuffle and the harsh screeching of that red door as it inched open. In the unearthly silence that followed a tall lanky man appeared. The light in the room seem to shrink back in fear lending a sinister atmosphere to the man's already deadly aura. I shivered as all the heat was sucked out of the room and replaced with an icy coldness.

He was few meters away from Dr. Levi before I caught a glimpse of his face and the blood fled from mine. He was darkness personified! Inky, spider-like, hair covered the majority of his face leaving just one eye, one red, slit-like, eye to peak through.

My heart that had been going wild since I woke up strapped to the table came to a complete standstill.

It was real! Every dream, no every nightmare, was real!

My heart roared back to life thundering in my chest and squeezing a terrified scream through my strangled throat.

Both men turned laser eyes on me and to my dismay all four eyes were now blood red slits that seemed to gleam at my near mindless terror.

"Shut up! You foolish girl. We are all family here. This is Dante, your brother. Unlike you, he is a failed experiment."

At his words, my screams turned hysterical and I gasped for breath as my mind tried to piece his words together. *That, is that what I am turning into?! Oh God! Oh God! I-I...* A new wave of despair, disbelief, and dismay crashed over me.

A malicious grin slid onto the doctor's face and he walked over to me. "Oh come now little one, I know you've realized it by now. The hunger pangs that never seem to be satisfied by just food, the sensitivity to light, the throbbing of your gums, and that overwhelming urge to rip into anyone who pisses you off.

No? What about the astounding super strength and the need to be one with nature in the most primal way? Even though the werewolf genes are practically indelible, I hope you will ignore the compulsion. The idea of you turning into a mutt repulses me."

Silence was the only response he got from me. His words had robbed me of…every thought. I couldn't speak. I couldn't breathe. Even my heart was refusing to beat.

"You my darling are turning into exactly what I created you to be. A vampire werewolf hybrid." A vicious grin was plastered on his face when he delivered the last blow to my mind. As the words bounced around the room, I blacked out.

*****

"Tsk, what a weak little girl." With a look of disgust marring his handsome face Titus turned away from his prized creation and glanced at his failure. The atmosphere around them turned even deadlier than before as he demanded an answer.

"Why hasn't she turned into my weapon yet? What did the doctor say?" There was a pause and Dante slowly opened his mouth.

"M-Ma-Master, t-t-he Do-doc-doctor..." apart from the werewolf gene never manifesting fully in Dante he also had a speech delay and a congenital eye disorder.

Impatience dashed across Titus' face as he listened to his useless prototype. With a move swifter than the flash of lightning, Titus grabbed Dante by the throat and pulled him close. With a careless flick of his hand and a savagery born of pure evil Titus unsheathed his fangs and tore into Dante's throat. As he gulped the spewing blood images of Dante's not so polite chat with the doctor that helped him create his precious weapon came streaming into Titus' mind.

He watched with growing pleasure and smiled around the flesh in his mouth as he watched Dante torture the old man by driving his thumb nail into the man's leg until it met bone. The scream of pain and desperate plea to be free was almost too delicious to ignore but he was drinking for a purpose so with a bit of reluctance he fast forward through Dante's memories until the answer he had been searching for came to him.

It was so obvious, yet he had missed it. *His little prize had to die!* What was rebirth without death?

A heinous smile spread across his devilish face. In that moment, he was the bearer of death, the harbinger of destruction, and with the death of this creature the ruler of all.

Chapter 15

Death Comes For Us All

Just as Aria and I disembarked from the taxi in front of what could only be described as a mini modern palace a breathtakingly handsome man opened the door and walked out. "Hello Tianna. Please come in. My name is Keith. Josiah sent me." Every thought left my mind at the sight of the exquisitely beautiful man before me.

Everything about him oozed of royalty. From the halo like hair, soft hazel eyes, clean shaven jawline, to his imposing height that made a mockery of my husband's stature.

In my daze I allowed him to take my hand and lead me into the house. The instant I stepped over the threshold I was met with such opulence that my breath caught in my throat. It made perfect sense. There was no way a man that exuded royalty would be surrounded by anything less.

The beautiful hotel I just left seemed cheap in comparison to the lavishness of this home. There was a chandelier in the hallway which I just knew was made of pure diamond. Millions of dollars' worth of artwork by Picasso and Rembrandt hung on every wall and the tiled floor had to have been imported from Italy. It all screamed multi-trillion dollar rich. *Just who was this guy and how did Josiah know him?!*

"Ana...Tianna." A velvety smooth voice called my name tugging my attention from the surroundings back to him.

"I know this is a bit much for you but I need you to focus and tell me all you can about Nicolette, her parents, the car they drove away in, and the name of the doctor they were going to see."

At his words, an influx of anxiety and worry for Nikki churned through me. That's right; I wasn't here to look at art. I was here to get help saving my friend.

In as little time as possible I spilled everything I could think of that would help Nikki. Keith listened with ferocious intensity. The looks on his face vacillated between calmness and fury. As soon as I was finished he nodded and another man appeared out of nowhere and was by my side in a flash. I was so startled I almost dropped a sleeping Aria.

Keith frowned at the man and they exchanged a meaningful look that I didn't understand. "Okay my dear. Severino will help you to get settled in." He paused and seemed to debate with himself for a moment before leveling a piercing gaze at me.

"Don't worry about Nikki, anymore. I will find her and bring her back to you." With that, he turned and exited the room leaving my heart aflutter with admiration and relief.

*****

I had to walk away at the pace of a human even though the blood from my recent feed rushed through me making me want to bound through the streets. Outrage and a need for violence thumped in my veins. The silly little girl I helped to escape a few years ago had somehow gotten herself into a lot of trouble. I remember the scared look on her face when she saw her parents at the airport in Chicago. Back then I hadn't been able to find out much about her other than what her parents did and who they worked for, P.O.A.H.

In the last five decades P.O.A.H. had been taking over the scientific field specifically anything involving genetics. They had gone as far as kidnapping vampires and werewolves. All in the name of protecting humans. It was getting out of control. Just recently a whole village in southern Italy was eliminated by assassins and after an exhaustive investigation it turned out that P.O.A.H was behind it. Titian, one of the oldest vampires alive had warned us in last year's meeting that there was more afoot than just humans getting lucky but his admonition had been shot down.

I hated to admit it, but I had been one of the people that voted to ignore him. Now, from the story Tianna told me it was possible that Nikki was being turned into a vampire without her knowledge.

It took roughly 30 minutes to track down Nicolette and her parents. The family sedan was discovered wrecked on the highway. Mr. and Mrs. Winspere were laying among the mangled steel, their bodies drained of blood. The scene wreaked of foul play and Nikki was nowhere to be found.

It took another half hour to find the execution team and extract her whereabouts from them. By the time I got a location it was close to 11p.m. and my temper had risen to an all-time ungodly high.

It was unclear who, but someone other than P.O.A.H knew about Nicolette's abilities and had swiped her from under their noses. Whoever it was had been meticulous. My team had threatened and beaten the kidnappers mercilessly until it became clear that the only thing they knew was where the boss was holed up.

I waved my hands and the small army surrounding me prepared themselves for battle. There was no telling what we were walking into and it was better to be prepared.

*****

Keith had been so caught up in making plans to rescue Nicolette that he failed to realize that Tianna had been eavesdropping and overheard the location.

While no one was paying attention, she kissed Aria, handed her to the nanny, and snuck into one of the many vans, filled with soldiers and weapons, just before it pulled out the driveway.

*****

He had waited almost two millennia for this moment and it was finally here. With hawk-like eyes Titus watched as Dante deftly mixed the hypocloride concoction.

As soon as it was ready, he snatched it and walked to the table where the little girl was strapped down. He woke her up with a vicious slap to the face.

He would not allow her to sleep through her rebirth! It would be an insult to all his hard work. Plus he wanted her to see the moment she become his weapon.

*****

Nikki regained consciousness with a startled cry and immediately wished she hadn't. Dr. Levi was standing over her and by the malevolent look on his face whatever he had planned was not going to be pleasant.

"Are you ready my dear? The time for your awakening is here! As soon as I inject this into your bloodstream you will die and, if you are lucky, your supernatural blood will kick in. If not well…you'll just be dead; won't you? Do me a favor darling? Don't die!"

The fierceness in his voice seem to spread to his eyes and explode around him as he forbade Nikki from dying.

With a swiftness that shocked her once again, and reminded her that she was at the mercy of a monster, Titus stuck the needle in her arm.

A firm knock rang through the room scaring Nikki more than the syringe jutting out of her arm. A man dressed in a black suit stepped through the door and bowed before stepping closer to Dante and then to Titus.

He whispered something in the doctor's ear and the temperature in the room plunged once more becoming icy cold as the aura of death enveloped him.

"GET RID OF THEM!"

"We are trying sire but they are ripping through our forces like they are water. I think they are from the Royal Guards.

At the mention of the Royal Guards a cold grin spread across Titus' face and blossomed into maniacal laughter.

"Those weaklings? Don't let me down boy. Kill them all!" The guttural utterance of his words left everyone quaking in fear. In seconds the man was gone.

Turning to look at the frail girl who would soon be able to massacre entire armies at the drop of a hat, Titus walked over to her in slow measured steps. He was enjoying the way her heart galloped and then fluttered alternatively as he drew closer.

"Nothing to worry about my darling once you awaken you will take out everyone who dares to oppose me.

"Hold it right there!" The door banged opened and Tianna stepped through holding a gun. "Get away from her."

*****

I was shocked at the sudden appearance of my best friend and even as I uttered a warning I knew it was too late. "N-NO, NO! RUN T, RUN!"

One minute the doctor was smiling like a cat that caught a canary and the next second he was standing behind Tianna.

She never saw him coming and Titus twisted her head in one a swift movement. The snapping of her neck echoed throughout the small room.

I froze as Titus brushed his hands together and stepped over Tianna's body like she was nothing but a pesky bug. "Tsk, tsk. A human has no place here."

I watched his mouth form the words but couldn't hear them. There was a roaring in my ears and a growing wave of horror rose up, threatening to crash over me. Instead something within me seemed to burst and flow through my body. With a hard yank I pulled one hand out of the restraints and then the other.

"Oh yessss, yes! You are almost there! Your scent is getting stronger." Titus crowed gleefully.

I felt detached from my body watching the fury grow and spread inside me at the sight of the body on the floor and the man who had, with no reaction, dispatched my friend like she was trash.

Just as I got ready to move he stood before me and smiled sweetly. "Ha-ha, if looks could kill. Not to worry sweetheart in just a second all those feelings will disappear." With a quick motion, he emptied the long forgotten syringe into my arm and then all hell broke loose.

*****

"Do you smell that? Jameel, track that scent." My forces and I had been steadily dispatching vampires and humans alike for the last ten minutes and we still had not found Nikki. It wasn't until we turned a corner that I picked up her scent intertwined with that of a very familiar human. I hissed in frustration as I connected the scent to the owner; Tianna. How the hell had she gotten here?

Unease threaded up my spine and I increased the ferocity of my attacks. This was no place for a human and Tianna had waded into the thick of it.

The deeper into the fortress we got the stronger Nicolette's and Tianna's scents became until they were centered behind a door. As I was about to open it a sharp battle cry alerted me to an attack.

Staggering back hastily, I was able to avoid what would have been a fatal stab to my heart. I swung around expecting to take out my attacker only to meet air.

I frowned. That should have been impossible. There was no way a normal vampire could completely evade me. Even my master had a hard time countering my attacks when I was this focused.

A ferocious battle ensued between me and the attacker. He was unreal! Faster than anyone I had ever encountered. He had such precise movements that I was forced to be overly vigilant and cautious with my every move.

Deranged laughter spread through the hall distracting the boy in front of me for a split second which was just enough time for me to tear out his throat. He reacted as quickly slashing down on my wrist with a wooden blade that split my skin. In his dying moment he mouthed two words, "too late."

An unknown feeling bloomed in my heart as I burst through the door to the ringing sound of a heart monitor flat-lining.

There she laid, the sweet girl I had rescued five years ago, the same beautiful dark skin, red cupid lips, and high cheek bones. All that was missing was that gorgeous smile that, until now, I hadn't realized I had missed over the last couple of years. It was something to behold…wild, mischievous and brimming with promise.

It was all gone! She was dead! Standing over her body was a man emanating an energy that belonged in a mad house.

He ignored me even as I made a bee line for him. I was steps away from when he turned swiftly and delivered a hard stinging back hand that drove me to my knees.

He turned to look at me and in his moss-colored eyes was interest and amusement. "Hmm…not bad! That hit was meant to kill you. The fact that you survived it means you are not one of those weaklings. We will see each other soon." In a blink, he was gone. Everything in me wanted to chase after him but I couldn't leave Nikki's body alone. Not in a place like this.

Epilogue

The stench of blood hung heavy in the air but there was only one person on my mind; my mate! Keith had yet to check-in since leaving last night and I was beside myself.

Everywhere I looked there were body parts; both human and vampire but I saw through all of them. All I was interested in seeing was my mate.

Since I had gotten off the helicopter there was an awful feeling, that I couldn't decipher, in the pit of my stomach.

My nose found her before my eyes could. Happiness flooded my system until I saw how pale she looked. The natural glow of her deep golden colored skin seemed to be seeping from her with every passing moment.

Focusing my auditory senses I listened for her heart beat but was met with silence. There was nothing! Nothing at all! Indescribable agony ripped through me.

All there was, all I good see and feel, was agony! In a flash, I ripped her from Keith's hand and started CPR. I couldn't…I couldn't breathe; not when my mate, my one and only, was gone.

"Josiah, we have to go! There are too many bodies. We can't be found around this. Come brother. We will bring her body and give her a proper burial."

As he spoke, a roar rumbled through me. Spilling forth with such intensity that everyone around us with sensitive hearing was driven to their knees.

Caught up in expelling my pain, I almost missed the answering roar of the woman in my arms. She displayed unbelievable agility as she sprung to the ground.

"WHERE IS HE?" the guttural sound of the woman in front of us astonished everyone. "I SAID, WHERE IS HE?!"

She moved so swiftly that she became a blur appearing to be everywhere at once. We couldn't see her but we heard the frenzied rampage as she bombed through walls and tore down doors.

"Everyone out! She's going to bring the whole place down." Keith's bellow brought us all to our senses and we streaked out the building as quickly as we could.

No one said a word. None of us knew what to say. The woman I was crying over only moments before was now a deadly tornado bringing everything around her to its knee.

Just as the walls of the fortress began to crumble Nicolette emerged with a body in her arms. Her head was bowed and grief radiated off her in waves. It wasn't until she raised her head and our eyes locked four that I understood.

The scent that had been wafting through the building since I stepped in finally made sense. It was coming from her and it was no longer human nor was it fully werewolf.

One of her eyes glowed gold while the other glowed red. She was both werewolf and vampire and so much stronger than either.

What Readers Are Saying

"Your writing is very descriptive in this. You have a unique elegance with your words that forms these fantastic sentences that are just gorgeously rendered."

-K. Setty

"I'm anxious to find out what happens."

-N. Grande

"Love it, Love it. Can't wait to read the rest of the series!"

-B. Ryan

"The plots is surprising and refreshing a twist to the werewolf vampire dichotomy."

-A. Abina

"Leaves you wanting more and pleasantly open to possibilities"

-L. Jadis

About the Author

Saugia N. Smiley is a talented African Caribbean author who was born and raised in St. Catherine, Jamaica.

As a teenager, she immigrated to the United States and for 6 years called Boston, MA home before putting down roots in Houston, TX.

Saugia is an avid traveler whose first "real" job after formal schooling was as a flight attendant with a major US airline.

Her writings are loosely based on her childhood, her life experiences, and her vivid imagination.

Saugia is driven by a passion to see more publications that feature dark skinned people in a leading and positive role. Her life's motto is "just because it's never been done before doesn't mean it cannot be done."

Connect with the Author

Instagram
darkskin_writer

Facebook
Smiley's Dark Skin Books

Website
https://darkskinwriter.com/

Email
smilesdarkskin@gmail.com

Upcoming Titles

Weathered; *June 16, 2019*

The Circle of Seven; *September 1, 2019*

CPSIA information can be obtained
at www.ICGtesting.com
Printed in the USA
FFHW020745230519
52611136-58103FF